P9-CJF-105

To Jackie

Waiting
IN THE WINGS

Gene Green

Waiting
IN THE WINGS

Geene Rees

Block Books Publishing

Waiting in the Wings

After You've Gone, Music by Turner Layton, lyrics by Henry
Creamer. Public Domain. Published in 1918.

Bill, Music by Jerome Kern, lyrics by P.G. Wodehouse. Public
Domain. Published in 1917.

I Don't Want to Get Thin by Sophie Tucker. Public Domain.

ISBN: 978-0-997670219

Library of Congress Control Number: 2016909540.

Contact: reesmktg@gmail.com

Cover design: James Jimi
Strand Theater Illustration: Judith Mattingly
Cover photo: iStock, eclipseart:
Book design: Jim Shubin—www.bookalchemist.net

Printed in the United States of America.

*To the memory of my grandmother,
with love.*

Introduction

Hidden in a compartment of my grandmother's bottom dresser drawer was an old scrapbook. Pressed inside were photographs of a beautiful young woman and hundreds of newspaper clippings about vaudeville shows and the movie industry. This is how I learned about my great aunt, Ruby Adams. As a child, I combed through the items that chronicled her life as a vaudeville headliner—her success and her tragedy.

In the heyday of the 1920s, motion pictures were replacing vaudeville as the number one form of public entertainment. Studios such as Paramount, Fox, and Loew's were buying up theaters like postage stamps in an effort to control the distribution of their silent pictures. In San Francisco, there was one first-rate theater downtown, on Market Street, that continued to offer vaudeville.

One night in January 1925, while getting ready

to take the stage at the Strand Theater, an incident occurred that changed Ruby's life. In 1925, her story was headline news, yet I could find no biographies or memoirs written about her. Ruby Adams' life and her career as a singer, dancer, and actress had been forgotten. That's when I realized I had to tell her story.

It was my grandmother's memories that brought this tale to fruition. Her love and devotion to her younger sister drove me to search for the truth of what happened to Ruby on that fateful night at the Strand Theater.

It took more than ten years to write *Waiting in the Wings*. This isn't the book I thought I would write. I'd assumed I would craft a life-and-times biography, but the lack of historical records didn't let me tell that story. There was a court case, but all the court documents have disappeared—probably misplaced, but possibly destroyed. Ruby continued to work as a singer, yet all the recordings of her voice are gone too. Much has been written about the times, but very little on the life. My tale of Ruby Adams and the circumstances surrounding that night at the Strand has been woven from family lore, scrapbook memorabilia, newspaper clippings, and a tax-evasion case from 1940, which I uncovered in the U.S. National Archives.

While the story is grounded in history, this book is a work of fiction. It does, however, represent the closest possible likeness to my great aunt and the events that befell her. She was witty, clever, and brave, and with this novel I hope she will emerge from the wings and stand onstage once again.

◆

One

Ruby Adams rushed out through the revolving door of the St. Francis Hotel. The glass door had protected the elegant lobby from the brutal winter wind, and she was surprised when a blast of cold air hit her face. Fifty miles west of San Francisco a storm was approaching, and in a few hours, it would drop more than two inches of rain on the city.

On the sidewalk, the doorman, a trench coat covering his snazzy green uniform, noticed her immediately. Her eyes were large and almond-shaped, dark brown with tiny flecks of gold; with her dimpled chin, they were her most striking feature. Just a couple of inches over five feet tall, she had a deceptively fragile appearance. Ruby possessed a great deal of confidence, which was evident as she stood at the top of the hotel's broad stairway, peering at the veil of clouds as they rolled eastward. Late for the theater, she had no time to dawdle. And yet she hesitated.

"Evening, Miss Adams."

"Evening, Burt. You see any taxicabs?" Ruby asked, tucking her dark hair into a fashionable felt camel-colored hat. His hand flew up to the shiny brim of his cap and, with a swift wipe of his forefinger, he replied, "No, this weather is snarling traffic around the square."

"Well, I'm going to be late for my rehearsal if I don't dash. Wish me luck."

"Miss Adams, the world's your oyster. I should ask you for luck," he told her, smiling.

Ruby laughed and straightened her shoulders, then snapped open her umbrella and stepped into the damp evening air. She was rarely late for the theater, and the Strand was eight blocks away. *Walk faster*, she told herself. She was twenty-eight years old and, thanks to the show's daily dance rehearsals, in terrific shape. She often walked to the Strand from the St. Francis, where she'd been living for the past three months. There was no better hotel in the city, centrally located on Union Square, with first-class amenities and a renowned French-schooled chef. Her room on the fifth floor overlooked the square, with its imposing hundred-foot-tall monument topped by a statue of "Victory." Many San Franciscan's knew that the model had been Alma de Bretteville Spreckels, while she still worked as a nude model for local artists, before she married one of the city's wealthiest citizens.

Unknown to the public, Ruby's room adjoined a suite occupied by another well-known local, John Davis. In fact, Ruby had been delayed by a series of telephone calls from a reporter—there was talk around town, he had said, that she and Davis were engaged to be married. Furthermore, a Stutz Bearcat motorcar belonging to Davis had been seen at the stage door of the Strand the previous night. Ruby was used to toying with the press. "I don't know where that idea came from," she told the reporter. "Maybe somebody can tell me? We are simply sweethearts!" The press wasn't buying it.

Ruby held her dark blue raincoat tight against her body as she moved through the throngs of shoppers and theatergoers buffeted by the wind. All the corner flower stands had closed for the day, leaving an array of crushed and wilted petals on the sidewalk. Ruby picked up the pace and wound her way down Mason toward Market Street, the three-mile-long diagonal slash from the Ferry Building, on San Francisco Bay, west to Twin Peaks. Lined with shops, theaters, office buildings and department stores, this broad thoroughfare was the heart of San Francisco. With the pavement shimmering under the yellow sodium-vapor lamps, it was clear where Market Street's nickname, Path of Gold, had come from.

Ruby's gait was light and effortless, graceful—she moved like a butterfly, the critics claimed. Jaywalking across Mason, Ruby nearly bumped into an expensive motorcar, whose passenger, smiled and waved. San Franciscans claimed the dark-haired beauty as their own. Born and raised in the city, Ruby had performed in local cabarets and theaters since she was a child; for the past year, she'd been a featured player with the Will King Follies. Ruby mouthed a polite "hello" and continued heading toward Market and the city's densest concentration of theaters.

Hollywood had been casting long shadows over Market Street. For the last five years, the movie business had been at war with vaudeville, and the war was heating up. Companies like Paramount and First National were buying up theaters everywhere, with the sole purpose of showing the movies the studios produced. Others were building expensive movie "palaces," their grandeur and luxury to be enjoyed by the masses as they watched the studio's latest moving pictures.

Up ahead, the flashing yellow marquee lights of the Loew's Warfield, the Cameo, and the Granada glowed in the mist. Ruby paused to study the Granada's elaborate Spanish-Revival architecture, a stark contrast to the tiny tobacco shop, with its carved wooden Indian, next door. Decorated inside and out with an Andalusian theme, the Granada was what the studios were calling an *atmospheric theater,* built by Herb Rothchild, a San Francisco attorney with a keen business sense, just four years earlier.

Now the theaters were pushing their way west, up Market Street, where the property was less expensive and access still easy via streetcar. In 1925, vaudeville was just a small annoyance, and the outcome seemed clear: Ruby would bet on moving pictures to win and hold their position until something else took their place. But tonight, she was performing at the Strand—the only large theater in a four-block radius to offer a mix of live entertainment and picture reels. The Will King Follies gave the people of San Francisco a *damn good show,* she thought. While billed as musical comedy, the Follies offered plenty of dancing, spectacle, and high jinx. High-class vaudeville is what they called it, and it was still popular in the city by the bay.

"These revues can't be gotten up in a hurry," Will King, the well-known showman and actor, often said. "They take time and money. These *crumb bums* in Hollywood are stealing my actors from underneath my nose. And what does the audience get? A flickering black-and-white image moving across the screen to some tinny piano music."

But after all his years in the business, King had begun to second-guess his instincts. In the past year, he'd spent upwards of fifteen-hundred dollars creating new acts, only to find the audience liked the old acts better. After rehearsals, he sometimes begged the Catholics in the cast to pray for a smooth opening. No one knew when vaudeville would be done for good.

Casting her worries aside, Ruby kept her mind on her first number, "Lotsa Papa," Papa being

Sweet Daddy Jack, a popular three-hundred-pound comedian. Her feet kept time with the rain as it pelted her umbrella. "Ba-dum, ba-dum," she sang. "Mmmm, I love your ba-dum." The show had been a hit; at last night's opening, they'd left the audience wanting more. Ruby could not imagine performing without an audience, hearing the applause and laughter, but as she headed to the theater, she realized she was not the first vaudevillian, nor would she be the last, to make the move to moving pictures.

Her agent had argued that he should tell King she would be leaving the show. But Will King was her friend. He had hired her years ago, and he'd taught her so much. *Timing is key! Adjust your tempo to the audience. Be prepared every time you approach the stage. The way you walk onto the stage, your style, how you bow, how you smile—they're all part of your act, kid.* Yes, it was only right for her to tell him.

Late last year, she had been courted by Famous Players-Lasky in Hollywood. Undeterred by her inexperience in the movie business, Jesse Lasky had said she looked good on film, and he made her an offer. She was a *new-era* woman and saw the decision as pragmatic, black-and-white: She was an actress who performed comedy well; the movie business was growing, and vaudeville was dying. Besides, she wanted to spend more time with John. The vaudeville circuit, demanding so much time spent on the road, was not conducive to good relationships.

"How do I *know* we should marry if we never spend more than one evening together?" she had told Davis just last night, dancing around the subject.

At the Warfield, where she could cross Market at one of the street's few traffic lights, she paused and lifted her gaze to the theater, once a three million-dollar vaudeville palace, now owned by Metro-Goldwyn-Mayer. After her performance at the Warfield in 1921, *The Wasp*, San Francisco's elite newspaper, had proclaimed Ruby a convincing soubrette in John Drew's *The Butterflies*, dubbing her Butterfly.

"Ruby! Break a leg!" A young man, climbing into a uniform-delivery truck carrying two thick jackets with decorative gold epaulettes, waved. She managed a wink as she took shelter from the rain under the awning of the marquee. Finally, the stoplight changed color and she trotted across

Market, past rows of black automobiles with big headlamps and high-pitched horns, and down cobblestoned Stevenson Alley.

The Strand was an L-shaped building that took up half a block. The steel structure, with its buff brick and ornate renaissance detailing, had been built in 1910—just four years after the great earthquake and fire destroyed half the city—to survive any quake that might follow. The auditorium, with its rows of blue velvet clamshell-backed chairs, plush burgundy-carpeted aisles, warm wood paneling, and gilded sconces, was as elegant as any in town, and the rest of the theater offered everything needed for a vaudeville show: orchestra pit, a wing at each side of the stage, trapdoors for special effects, a high, roomy fly space for scenery, ropes, and riggings.

As Ruby climbed the narrow metal stairs at the back of the theater to the STAGE DOOR, she heard a sound. A few paces from the door in the shadowy pathway, a young stagehand in a gray raincoat huddled close to the trashcans. Even from a distance and in the dim light from the gooseneck lamp at the door, Ruby could see the silhouette of a flask of *lightning* or *smoke* or some other type of bootlegged liquor in his hand.

Unaware, or unconcerned, that he was being watched, the stagehand bent one leg against the building, leaned back, and took a long swig. This wasn't the first time she'd noticed him in the alley before a show. But he seemed to know what to do backstage. Ruby closed her umbrella and grabbed the knob of the heavy stage door. As soon as the metal door clicked open, she slipped into the warmth of the theater.

Inside, the lights were low and the music was loud. With only two hours till curtain, the stage attendant looked relieved. "Evening, Miss Adams. I was beginning to think you lost your way." Walter wasn't a talkative fellow, but he felt personally responsible for the safety of the female performers and kept a watchful eye on the backstage entrance.

As the door clanged shut, Ruby said playfully, "How could I lose my way? You know I slipped in that very door when I was young, just to see what a real backstage looked like."

"Yes, well, if I'd been here that night, there'd be no way you could have snuck through that door."

"Yes, I guess I was fortunate."

"You better get going, Miss Adams. You know what Mr. King says. 'If you're early, you're on time. If you're on time, you're late, and if you're late, you're fired!'"

Ruby could see Will King barking out orders for the electrician. "I'd better get down to my dressing room double-quick then."

"Well, *youse* need to know the duet's been scratched. Your partner Miss Valerie's sick."

As Ruby slipped off her dripping coat, she gazed out at the stage and the chorus girls pounding out jazz time. Rehearsals were winding down. She turned back to Walter and said, "Well, I don't see that as a bad thing. I much prefer a solo. Listen, if Mr. King asks for me, tell him I was delayed by the press. He'll like that."

"That man likes free publicity, that's for sure."

"How's the house tonight?" Ruby asked.

"You needn't worry. Sold out!" Walter said, sitting down again on his wooden captain's chair and picking up a newspaper. The theater's contract with Will King stated that he would gross sixty percent of all ticket receipts and the theater forty percent. So long as the revenues were good, the Will King Follies was guaranteed a long run.

Ruby rushed across the passageway to a stairway that led downstairs to the dressing rooms. A heavyset man in a tuxedo was attempting to climb up the stairs to the stage level when he suddenly bent over and gasped. It was Sweet Daddy Jack, his jowly face and bald head dripping with sweat.

"My goodness, Jack! You should take the elevator," Ruby said, pulling a handkerchief embroidered with a rose from her coat pocket and handing it down to him.

"Thank you, darling. You and I agree, but my doctor advises me otherwise. He says I need to get more exercise."

Jack dabbed the perspiration from his brow as he confronted the next step.

"Ruby, I'm glad you've arrived! I daresay what we'd do without you. Will was worried you'd gone off to join the circus. I told him that was impossible, that you loathe animals. And anyhow, a star never abandons a company after favorable reviews!"

"I guess our little act stopped the show last night."

"You're at the top of your game, and we had some of the best notices in the newspaper this morning," Jack said, wiping more sweat from his brow.

Ruby thought the doctor should restrict Sweet Daddy's diet instead of suggesting exercise. Panting heavily, Jack asked for her help, and Ruby held out her small hand. His fat fingers took hold of hers and he pulled himself up the remaining steps, leaving the scent of bay rum and tobacco in his wake.

The atmosphere was tense in the hallway. You could hear nervous giggles, temper tantrums, and shouts of frustration from the chorus and cast. And yet all knew the show would miraculously come together in less than two hours' time.

A moment later, Ruby stood at the threshold of her dressing room with her hands on her hips. "Good lord. What the hell? Maestro!" Lying peacefully in front of her door was a dead mouse. A cat that lived in the theater had taken a liking to Ruby, though what Maestro saw in her, she couldn't fathom. Jack was right; she didn't like animals, especially cats, because they made her eyes water. With one brush against her leg, a cat could ruin her makeup. Now this one was leaving her small dead critters.

At the beginning of her career, Ruby would have

viewed a dead mouse as a bad omen. Now she took little notice of omens, good or bad. Still, something would have to be done, she thought. She stepped over the mouse, opened the dressing room door, and closed it before the cat could follow.

Shrugging off her street clothes and hat, Ruby slid into the red silk Chinese robe that hung from a hook on the dressing room door, relaxing as she felt the silk against her skin. She'd grown to love beautiful things: silks, fine linens, jewelry, Champagne. As she walked over to the ballet barre, she pushed aside a stack of books and sheet music. Ruby had completed only eight years of school, but she read whenever she got the chance. Interested in numbers and musical composition, she had taught herself to read and write music and play the piano; she learned dance steps easily. Swinging a leg up onto the barre, she gently stretched her lower back and hamstrings.

When her body felt sufficiently warmed up, she went to the room's little sink, filled a small bowl with water, and began her nightly ritual at the vanity table. After years of performing in vaudeville, Ruby had perfected a system that maximized efficiency; she could get ready in less than ten minutes. She'd have to hurry tonight, though, because the wind had played havoc with her hair, and it would have to be reset. Thank goodness John would pick her up after the show tonight, and she wouldn't have to battle for a cab.

She snapped open a small leather trunk with her

initials imprinted in gold and smoothed out a white towel on which she placed her comb, brush, and the bowl in a neat row. Quickly separating thick strands, she positioned bobby pins and duckbill clips to style her hair. As the finger wave took shape, she became aware of an intoxicating scent from the corner of the room. White roses were especially difficult to buy in winter, and someone must have spent a pretty penny on these, she thought. She uncrossed her legs and rose to look at the card when there was a knock on the door.

"It's Will."

Will King stood in the doorway, in the flaxen wig and baggy trousers held up by bright red suspenders that he would wear for his opening monologue.

"You found me," she said, tightening the belt of her robe around her tiny waist.

"Yes, I am clever that way. I thought I'd come down to see if you need anything," he said in a gentle voice.

Ruby walked over to the vanity table and sat down. "For starters, you can have that mouse removed from outside my door. I don't know how Maestro knows this is my dressing room, but I really prefer my admirers to leave me gifts at the stage door." Ruby did not want for Stage-Door Johnnies and others who lingered at the back-stage door.

"It's funny—opening night's usually pure agony," Will said. "Everything goes haywire. Actors are schvitzing and their greasepaint melts. But last night, we got luck. No problems. Today's another kettle of fish. A leaky roof and burned-out lighting gels. The chandelier we use in the burglar skit crashed to the stage. This old girl is showing signs of age," he said, referring to the theater.

Ruby arched her eyebrows. "Oh, dear. Will, don't you ever get tired of working the circuit—all the traveling, the rooming houses, the old theaters and hotels?"

"Ha." He shook his head. "To live on the circuit is such pleasure! Speaking of admirers, how's your restaurateur?"

"Grandpa? He's just fine. We're hosting one of those boozy teas at the Aladdin Tea Room after the show tonight, if you and Claire care to join us. Mrs. Lo is making her famous spaghetti!" Ruby said with a glorious smile.

The first time King had seen Ruby, she was smiling like that. That was almost twelve years ago, and he had hired her on the spot. Men had always flocked to her like moths to a candle, and it had surprised him when she began dating John Davis. He was well known, successful, and rich, not without charm, but he was more than fifteen years her senior and her pet name for him was Grandpa.

"Maybe we will," Will said. "The wife loves Mrs. Lo's spaghetti!"

"Mmmm, she's not alone!"

"Listen, we sold out tonight! Nine of the ten critics here last night gave us rave reviews. Not bad for a cold winter night!"

"What do you think happened with that tenth critic? Did he nod off after the burglar skit?" Ruby asked with a mischievous grin.

"Ha! Listen, your double's been scratched. Valerie's sick. We'll need to do a last-minute change-a-roo. I'd like an elaborate number, but we have this problem with the backdrops; only three are working, and the scenic artist says it's too late to paint a new one. I was thinking 'Gwan with It,'" he said.

Will loved that song, but Ruby felt it was a little schmaltzy. It didn't have the sophistication she wanted to convey. After a pause, Ruby said, "What if I sing "After You've Gone"? That way, we can just use the black scenic drop."

"Swell idea! It's a simple song with lots of emotion. The audience loved it in Seattle."

King pulled a sheaf of papers from his oversize pants and held them out to her. "Here, take a peek. We're givin' out a photo souvenir to the womenfolk tonight."

Ruby took the studio portrait and studied it. She was sitting looking up at the camera, mouth closed to hide a slight overbite, her hands folded on her lap and her legs peeking out from a chiffon ruffled skirt.

"You've outdone yourself. You really should think about giving one to Maestro, too. You can tack it over his little hidey hole," she said as she handed back the photograph. Ruby adjusted a bobby pin as her voice lost its teasing tone. "Listen, there's something I want to tell you, Will."

"What is it, kid?" Will asked as he straightened his wig.

"In March, you know, my contract's up...."

"Oh, don't worry. I'll have the agency take care of that."

It wasn't the reply she wanted to hear.

"It's not that. I'm...not going to renew," she told him.

Will whistled. "Holy mackerel! Are you playing me?"

"N-no," she replied, stumbling on her words. "I'm going to do a picture."

Will considered the long-stemmed white roses in the corner of the room. He walked over and looked at the card. They were from a florist located at Hollywood Boulevard and Vine.

"Kid, you're a singer and a dancer. Your talent will be wasted on the silver screen."

"I'm not getting any younger, Will. Anyhow, I'm set to do a comedy."

He curled his thumbs around his suspenders. "It's true that when you dance, laughter comes out."

They both had a good laugh recalling the poorly worded review she had gotten early on.

"Hell, I don't have to tell you that I wish you luck, but damn those movie bums. I hope you ain't working for that crumb bum at Fox!"

"No, for that crumb bum at Famous Players-Lasky."

Will nodded. "He's a good fellow."

"Yes. He is."

Just then, a ching-a-ling rang out from the piano upstairs, followed by an off-beat ragtime.

Will looked up at the ceiling. "The boys are gettin' restless."

"So it's settled?"

"No! You and I will discuss this later. I've got to talk to the conductor and see if he has the sheet music for 'After You've Gone.' Ha," he laughed humorlessly, "that's ironic, isn't it?"

Ruby watched his shoulders drop as he turned toward the door. "Will?"

"Yes?"

"Make sure that chorus boy—you know the one with the blond hair? Make sure he wears a jockstrap tonight."

Will looked back at his friend and shook his head in amusement. "Oy vay! You're a one, that's for sure. I'll have everyone ready in ten."

—⁓—

The rain was increasing as Basil Knoblock took one last swig of gin, capped the flask he always had with him, and shoved it into his newly polished ankle boot. It was time to get back to work. It was Basil's job to run the fly system, which controlled the curtains, the scenery, and all the backdrops used in the show. He felt especially powerful controlling the line set, wrapping the rope around the pin-rail cleat to secure the sandbag whose weight raised the curtain.

Brushing pass Walter at the door, he heard his name called as he looked at his pocket watch. "Basil!"

"Yes, sir?"

It was Bill Finck, the theater manager, standing next to the callboard. "There's some work we want you to attend to at the front of the theater."

"I was just about to check the riggings, sir."

"Nuts, you should have done that already. You're needed in the lobby! One of the radiators isn't working."

Basil didn't argue with his boss. "Yes, sir." When was the last time he'd checked the riggings? His memory was a little foggy. He'd have to get to the fly loft as soon as he finished with the radiator.

———

At the vanity table, Ruby looked at herself in the mirror and stuck out her tongue. "Well, that's done. Are you proud of yourself, you horse's ass?"

She picked up a jar of Pond's cold cream and began massaging the cream into her porcelain skin, concentrating her efforts around her eyes. With charcoal eye shadow, she accentuated the downward tilt of her almond eyes. Starting at the cupid's bow, she wrapped a cherry-red lipstick around her lips for a bee-stung look. As Ruby stepped into a black sequined gown that fit her like a glove, she heard the conductor working on orchestration for the new song, "After You've Gone." Something was wrong with the middle C on the piano, and the pianist was doing his best to work around it. She checked her hair and makeup once more and hurried out.

At the top of the stairs, she heard actors shouting their lines as the crew ran back and forth, from stage left to stage right and back again. Soon she was standing offstage in the wing, next to the black curtains known as *blacks*.

"Where'd you like your spike, Miss Adams?" a young stagehand asked. He held a roll of tape in his hand.

"Same as last night! Where the sound is perfect—center-left of heaven and two steps in front of the devil."

The young man's face turned beet red as the musicians laughed.

"Oh, hell, I'll show you." With that, she stepped to the center of the stage and walked six feet upstage, pointing with her foot to the spot. He walked over and placed the T-shaped spike mark downstage and ran off.

Ruby looked down at the orchestra. "Maestro, if you've fixed that middle C, you can give me some warmup music."

The conductor peeked over his pince-nez glasses. "You've a remarkable ear, darling." He nodded and turned to the orchestra. "Settle down, boys. You heard her! Let's give the little gal what she wants."

Ruby glanced up at the lighting technician and motioned. As the spotlight lit up the patch of stage around the spike, Ruby began humming loudly. When the brass instruments burst into a swinging rhythm in a minor key, her low-heeled shoe, with its dancer's strap across the instep, tapped out a four-four beat.

An unbridled joy came over her, and in her seductive, self-possessed way, Ruby began a slow, snakelike vamp. Step, step, slide, step. Step, step, slide. Then she licked her thumb in a provocative gesture that hinted of sex. As she moved closer to the footlights, she called to the musicians wedged into the pit.

"That was fun. You've got a good rhythm going," she said with enthusiasm. "Are you ready to rehearse the new song?"

"One and two and...."

Looking out at the empty house, Ruby imagined each of the beautiful clamshell- backed seats filled with a fashionably dressed man or woman, each one staring at her as the trumpets played the first few bars of "After You've Gone."

"*Me, me, me, me-me, me-me.*" Ruby warmed up her voice, then, snapping her fingers, threw back her head and sang.

Now won't you listen honey while I say
How could you tell me that you're going away?

She glanced over at the conductor. "A little slower, Hermie, okay?"

Don't say that we must part

Don't break your baby's heart
You know I loved you for these many years
Loved you night and day
Oh honey baby can't you see my tears
Listen while I say

Ruby's voice was a mixture of honey and vinegar, filled with conviction as she sang to an empty seat in the second row.

After you've gone and left me crying
After you've gone, there's no denying
You'll feel blue, you'll feel sad,
You'll miss the dearest pal you've ever had
There'll come a time, now don't forget it
There'll come a time when you'll regret it
Some day when you grow lonely,
Your heart will break like mine and you'll want
me only
After you've gone, after you've gone away.

Many said that Ruby sang with a tear in her voice. Her tone was similar to that of Miss Bessie Smith, Queen of the Blues, but Ruby added a rough edge when she sang songs like "Hesitation Blues" or "You Better Keep Babying Baby."

Will King was in his usual place during rehearsals, downstage right, thumbs hooked around his suspenders. "Sharp movements, Ruby, that's right. Raise your eyebrows. Sing for the back row!"

She looked over at him and winked.

◆

Two

Ruby Adams was the youngest of ten children, and she'd made it clear from the start that she was a fighter. Family lore had it that she was pronounced dead at birth, only to "come back to life" almost ten minutes later.

She was always small in stature, and as a child, her appearance was unremarkable, her pale skin sometimes looking sickly against her unruly black hair. But her face showed signs of a beauty yet to come. It was a unique face, blending her Spanish and English ancestry, with a chin dimple and large, hooded eyes that she would learn to put to good use.

Dressed in hand-me-downs from her sisters, Ruby walked to the Jean Parker Grammar School, halfway up the Broadway hill, five mornings a week. Her teachers agreed that she had an uncanny memory and fervor.

Each afternoon, Ruby would return home via bustling Columbus Avenue, skipping past the

Italian bakery shops and delicatessens, saying hello to every shopkeeper in North Beach. Sometimes she would do a quick soft-shoe routine on the sidewalk at Washington Square Park before she turned eastward and marched up Telegraph Hill. At the top, she'd turn down an alley to the three-story wooden building in which she lived in a tiny apartment with her father and five siblings. Her mother had died of a heart attack, two brothers had succumbed to pneumonia, and the two eldest siblings had married and moved away.

Every afternoon, she would cut up an apple and break off a piece of bread and sit in front of the upright piano left by a previous tenant. Almost ten, Ruby already had dreams of performing onstage. The eighty-two keys of the piano challenged her mind. After she taught herself to read music and play, she'd sit at the piano for hours, composing music for dance contests. Her father earned barely enough for them all, so she and her sisters entered Cakewalk contests to earn extra money and keep food on the table. Ruby worked at her dancing, too, and local vaudeville producers were becoming aware of the girl and how well she did this high-stepping dance with its prancing movements.

For an hour, Ruby had the apartment to herself. Then her sisters would arrive home from high school, and it would be time to prepare dinner.

The morning of April 18, 1906, began like any other. At five a.m., Will Adams lumbered across the apartment, his well-worn underwear showing a bulging stomach, and opened the back door. The tin he left out for the birds was still full of sunflower seeds. How odd, he thought. Glancing at the thin thread of orange light above the East Bay hills, he began to sing in his beautiful tenor voice, a good-morning tune. Then he retreated to the kitchen and put on a pot of water for tea.

Ruby turned over in bed as she heard her father preparing for his daily trip to the Almaden Valley, sixty miles away, to purchase fruits and vegetables to sell in the city. At the washbasin, Will Adams steadied his hand on the porcelain and picked up his razor. With his gray hair and jowly cheeks, he looked every one of his fifty-four years.

Just as he lifted the razor, he heard a dozen crows frantically cawing, the cups and dishes in the cupboards rattling. A moment later, an invisible force of nature ripped through the structure, the piano keys echoing throughout the second-floor apartment, the chandelier swinging violently. The children were tossed across the room like playthings as the earth twisted violently. Bricks from the neighbor's chimney crashed through the bedroom window. By then, Ruby and her siblings were rushing down the stairs to the street.

A few minutes later, after the earth stopped trembling, the family stood on the sidewalk in their nightclothes, looking down on the rubble that had been their neighborhood. Above them, electrical wires were swaying eerily.

"It sounds like the fireworks," someone hollered.
"Look, there's smoke!"

In a daze, the family watched as fire jetted upward somewhere near the corner of Battery and Washington Streets. The fire spun and curled and grew surprisingly quickly. Ninety percent of the buildings in San Francisco were made of wood, and the fire department had no way of telling people that the city's water-distribution system had been shattered by the earthquake and was essentially useless.

Ruby and her family were able to stay in the apartment for two more days. On the third day, an officer with General Funston's army knocked on the door. The winds had shifted, he told them, and the fire was spreading. They had to leave immediately. Refugee camps were being set up in Golden Gate Park. The next day, all the wooden structures atop Telegraph Hill were gone.

Thursday, April 19, 1906
The Call-Chronicle-Examiner
Earthquake and Fire: San Francisco in Ruins
Death and destruction have been the fate of San Francisco

Shaken by a temblor at 5:13 o'clock yesterday morning, the shock lasting 48 seconds and scourged by flames that raged diametrically in all directions, the city is a mass of smoldering ruins. At six o'clock last evening, the flames, seemingly playing with increased vigor, threatened to destroy such sections as their fury had spared during the earlier portion of the day. Building a path in a triangular circuit from the start in the early morning, they jockeyed as the day waned, left the business section, which they had entirely destroyed, and skipped to the residence portions. After darkness fell, the homeless were making their way with their blankets and scant provisions to Golden Gate Park and the beach to find shelter. Downtown, everything is in ruins. Not a business house stands. Theatres are crumbled into heaps. Factories and commission houses lie smoldering on their former sites.

Eugene Schmitz, or "Handsome Gene," as everyone called him, was ill-equipped to be mayor of San Francisco. He was a musician who'd risen to power as president of the Musicians Union. He escaped City Hall whenever he could, preferring the warmth of his mansion in Burlingame when the summertime fog and wind became intolerable. His government was filled with graft and corruption. With a wink and a smile, he never failed to look the other way.

By 1906, three out of four of the city's four hundred thousand inhabitants were immigrants. The Irish made up the largest voting bloc. The Italians and Germans and Bavarian Jews had found great success as merchants, bankers, and politicians. More newly arrived immigrants from

Eastern Europe were pressing the older families from Ireland, France, and Germany.

And now the delicate fabric that held San Franciscans together was beginning to unravel. Many people had been left with nothing. "Anyone caught looting should not be arrested," said Mayor Schmitz, "but shot." Little looting occurred, yet martial law was declared at once, causing both the innocent and the guilty to be shot without a hearing. *Was someone looking for medical supplies a looter?* Many wondered. *What about someone looking for something to eat because his home was gone?*

Thousands of refugees settled in Golden Gate Park. Others fled to Oakland, San Rafael, and San Jose. Ruby's brothers set up their round military-provided tent alongside refugees who spoke different European languages. The expression on their faces, however, was the same, that of permanent shock. All had seen death on every street and every corner. Women, men, and animals lay crushed beneath the rubble.

Their refugee camp was about a mile from the ocean, on a patch of land that had good drainage and was sheltered by a grove of eucalyptus trees. It was originally inhabited by Chinese, whose cramped quarters had all but disappeared in the quake, until General Funston's military came along and sent them to a spot near the ocean. Later that day, a new sign appeared in the camp:
NO CHINESE ALLOWED.

Within weeks of arriving, Ruby and her sisters set up weekly talent shows featuring Cakewalk contests and comedy routines. Ruby was often seen striding to the middle of the camp, pounding on a tin can as if it were a drum, as men and women managed weary smiles.

"Ladies and gentleman, I'd like to perform the latest song written about our beloved city. Maestro, if you will," she said, turning to one of her brothers, also banging on a tin can. "From the ferries to Van Ness, you're a godforsaken mess. But the damndest finest ruins— nothin' more, nothin' less."

The lips on the Russians and Irish, Germans and Italians turned up, and everyone began to laugh and applaud.

"Ain't that the truth!" someone cried.

One night, a middle-aged man unveiled a Stradivari violin from a cloth bag and joined the young girl in song. From that night on, Ruby and the violinist entertained their homeless colleagues whenever they could. All agreed that the young girl lightened their hearts.

Turbulent living settled into routine. The aftershocks from the earthquake ceased. Those who had spent weeks worrying about family and friends accepted that they might never know what had happened to their loved ones. As the seasons changed, food became easier to find. Will Adams was able to get a job at the docks, where the horror amid the beauty of San Francisco impressed those aboard ships delivering supplies and construction materials for the city's reconstruction.

One foggy afternoon, Ruby and her two sisters ventured north of the park to The Chutes. A few years earlier, the Chutes Company had purchased a sandy parcel of land adjacent to Golden Gate Park and turned it into the largest pleasure resort in the country. The main attraction was a giant waterslide, where small boats would fly down a three-hundred-and-fifty-foot ramp and careen into a big lake. Despite the persistent foggy weather in the Richmond District, and the pall the earthquake and fire had cast over the city, The Chutes brought San Franciscans who could spare a nickel some joy.

Next to the amusement park sat a barnlike structure that housed the Chutes Theater. Before the earthquake, the theater had hosted band concerts and operas performed by opera students. Now the theater lay empty. Many musicians and other performers had left the city, and others had stopped coming, frightened by the thought of another earthquake. Finally, the Orpheum Circuit, which had lost its flagship theater in the disaster, booked the theater for three years, briefly renaming it the Orpheum.

Ruby and her sisters crossed D Street, passing a cluster of roadhouses and saloons newly built along the road, avoiding the rubble and construction materials on the sidewalks, and rushing past the two drunken men watching them as they ran toward 10th Avenue.

Less than a year earlier, they had seen Dockstader's Minstrels and a British pantomime troupe in this theater. It had been a turning point in Ruby's appreciation of the arts. Now Ruby climbed atop a wooden crate and peered into a grimy window. Her willingness to take risks no longer surprised her sisters. She'd stolen through the backdoor of many a theater. She'd entered talent contests and won by throwing her leg over her head. One night a few years back, she'd hopped on an old bicycle her brother Johnny had bought and ridden it down the street without any lessons.

Some families standing in makeshift kitchens in the middle of the street were watching the girls. Ruby jumped off the crate and said, "I'm going in, who wants to come?"

Edna, who was being courted by a well-to-do young man, shook her head. "I'm meeting Ray over at the circle swing."

"I'm coming with you," Mae said to Edna.

"Fine," Ruby replied as she tugged at the wide main door.

The door opened onto the lobby. She stood waiting for someone to scold her, but all she could see in the gloom were discarded ticket stubs and cigarettes, so she mounted the stairs to the balcony. When the newspaper stuffed in her shoes crackled, she adjusted a shoe on the landing, took hold of the banister, and climbed the remaining steps.

Ruby's eyes grew large as she peered over the brass railing to the empty stage. She sat down in the

nearest seat and inhaled the waxy smell of greasepaint as someone below commanded, "Positions!"

Two men and a big woman rushed downstage
from the left wing. The men wore white suits. The
woman was dark-skinned and dressed in a white
lace tea gown with long white gloves.

"And from the top," a man in the front row called.

The woman opened her mouth, and out came a
booming voice as she sang a rousing song with a
Southern accent. "I just love a Southern girl, if you
know what I mean?" one of the actors said,
elbowing the other in the ribs. The sound carried
well in the theater.

The dark-skinned woman stood looking at the
two men wearily, put her hands on her full hips,
and said, "I don't know what you mean. I'm not
Southern..." With a flourish, she removed a glove,
revealing pink skin underneath. "...I'm Jewish."
With a nod, she bade the men farewell and strode
offstage.

This caused Ruby to smile. Performers
occasionally used burnt cork or theatrical makeup
to darken their skin and perform in blackface.
Ruby never understood why.

The man in the front row gave a piercing whistle
as the black-faced woman returned to the stage,
smiling. "Grrreat! Sophie, say the line just like that
in the show, and the crowd will go wild."

A crack in Ruby's seat was cutting into the back
of her leg, so she moved slightly to ease the pain.

Suddenly, the seat split open and she fell to the ground.

"Who's up there?" the woman hollered.

For several seconds, the only sound was hammering, off in the distance. There was always construction going on in the city now. When Ruby realized her hand was touching a big wad of gum, she popped up.

"Me," she said, waving from the gallery.

"What are you doing up there?" the actress called to her.

"I'm studying, that's all."

"Studying? This ain't no schoolroom."

"There hasn't been any school since the quake. I've decided to become a dancer and singer."

"A dancer and singer, you say? Well, I'm tired of shouting. Get yourself down here, little one."

Summoning her confidence, Ruby worked her way down the carpeted staircase and up to the stage, finally standing before Sophie Tucker herself.

"You're a small little tot, but you've got what I call chutzpah!"

"You mean guts?"

Sophie put her hands on her thick waist and gave a belly laugh. "Yeah, how'd you know? You don't look Jewish."

"In the camps, people speak a lot of Yiddish."

"You live in the camps?" Sophie's heart was big and warm. She had given generously to the earthquake relief effort just the night before. The money would go to families living in the refugee camps, she'd been told. The little street urchin's shoes caught her attention, and Sophie hoped her donation would bring her a new pair. But for now, she supposed a singing lesson might cheer her. "How old are you?"

"I'm ten," Ruby said. "Tell me, why do you perform in blackface?"

Sophie sighed. "People say I'm too big and ugly to perform white. One day, someone painted my face with burnt cork and taught me how to be a coon shouter."

Ruby frowned.

"Coon shouting—it's a style of singing. Here, I'll show you."

Because many of the coon songs had risqué lyrics, Sophie settled on the first few bars of a song she had written.

Almost every day, I hear some kind friend say, Sophie, dear, you are much too stout.

Right away, they suggest the diet they think best. I wish they would cut it out.

I don't want to get thin. I don't want to get thin.
"Now you try."

Ruby plunged right in. "Almost every day, I hear some kind friend say, Ruby, dear, you are much too stout." She improvised a bashful grin after the word *stout* and Sophie clapped her hands joyfully.

"You're good! You should try out for some amateur nights."

Over the next two years, Ruby performed at

amateur nights throughout the city. The entertainment filled the public's passion for novelty and distraction. Part of the fun was using "the hook" to remove a disappointing performer from the stage, giving rise to the phrase "Get the hook."

Many restaurants, such as Tait's Café on Van Ness, offered amateur nights. Every Friday, five performers climbed the Tait's makeshift stage. Most would sing; others would juggle; a few danced a soft shoe. After an hour and a half of the crowd's fervent cheering and jeering, the manager presented the winner five silver dollars. As Ruby polished her act, the good audiences of San Francisco awarded her the prize money week after week. Her family sat along white flowered vines on the lattice-covered walls and voiced its approval.

But housing in San Francisco was extremely limited. Ruby and her sister Mae moved in with Edna, who had married her wealthy suitor. Will Adams rented a room not far from Golden Gate Park, but died of pneumonia a year after the earthquake. Ruby's brother Johnny married a nice Irish woman he'd met in the refugee camp and got a job at the *San Francisco Chronicle*. Her younger brothers had to leave the city to find work. Ruby wanted to continue performing, but she returned to school and studied for two more years.

In the summer of 1912, Ruby entered Techau Tavern, on Geary Street, and walked to the back of the restaurant. A rotund man with a pencil-thin mustache took a drag on his cigarette as he squinted at some sheet music. "You the kid with the letter from Sophie Tucker?"

"I am," she said, handing him her letter of introduction.

"It's just for tonight, or until our regular singer gets well."

"That's fine."

He looked at the letter. "Awright, let's see whatcha got."

Later, Ruby sang with the Paul Whiteman Orchestra. When Whiteman left for New York, Ruby looked for work in vaudeville. She met Will King at the Columbia Theater in Oakland. Most of the girls who auditioned for him didn't have a clue as to how to sing or dance; they seemed to feel they could get by on their looks. But Ruby had a sense of rhythm, and an effortless way of dancing, that proved to be just what King was looking for. Her singing had a nice bluesy style, with deep lows and tiny highs. And that smile....

"What's your name?" he asked in his gentle manner.

"Ruby. Ruby Adams," she told him, extending her small hand.

"You have some promising talent."

"Oh, thank you. I may not have the best voice in the world, but I think if I can keep in time with the music and pep things up a-plenty, I'll do all right."

King chuckled. "I'd like to book you for a show I'm producing."

He found she also had a flair for comedy and a strong work ethic. "The first to arrive and the last to leave," every stage-door attendant commented.

Ruby said more than once, "That damn earthquake dropped a load of sorrow all over San Francisco, but it led me to Miss Sophie Tucker, and that was the break I needed."

◆

Three

As the clock struck seven, thunder and lightning were moving into the Bay Area. In the lobby, Basil Knoblock knelt at the cast-iron radiator with a pipe wrench, trying very hard not to soil his clothing. Every few minutes, he turned the wrench to the right, then waited to see if the water would begin circulating through the pipes. He wiped his thick fingers and gave one last turn, and finally steam rattled from the pipes. A moment later, the banging began, and Basil smiled at the hissing sound of the radiator at work. Then he stood up and ran to the door marked AISLE 2.

He had to hurry. Soon the doors would open, and the people would be in a rush to get to their seats. He had to look over the prompt book and work through the scenic changes and curtain calls with the stage manager. He was the only stagehand who knew how to work the fly system. Lately, all management hired was boys who ogled and gawked at the chorus girls. Cheap labor, he told himself, isn't always worth the price.

The thought of not having enough time to check the fly loft unnerved him. The theater was fifteen years old, and all the equipment was aging. Before he opened the door to the auditorium, he wiped the pipe wrench with a rag and turned to look at the glass doors of the theater entrance.

"Bill!" he yelled to the theater manager, who was on the stairs leading to the balcony. "Crowd's getting angry. You'd better open up; I'm finished! And I need to get backstage!"

—⁓—

A "big-time" vaudeville production had a highly structured order. The entertainment began with the orchestra playing a selection of music from the show as the audience was being seated. Then came a short newsreel, followed by a monologue, a two-act skit, a "marital travesty," a musical number or soft-shoe routine, a clown or animal act if the company was big enough, a solo or duet, and finally, a batch of gorgeous chorines parading across the stage or down the runway.

Will King stood just offstage, arms crossed. He had watched Ruby rehearsing the new song with the appreciation it deserved. Then, reaching into his pants pocket for a handkerchief, he dabbed his eyes and muttered, "Damn the picture reels!" Perhaps it was inevitable that Ruby would move to Hollywood. Most of the good vaudevillians had:

Jimmy Durante, Buster Keaton, W.C. Fields. Hell, vaudeville stars were being used to sell pictures these days.

King was yanked from his thoughts by the floral perfume of *zaftig*, blonde-haired Clara LaVelle.

"Gonna be a good show tonight, Mr. King!" she said cheerfully, her New York accent even stronger than her perfume.

Will muttered something in Yiddish and stomped off down the passageway behind the stage. Clara gave little thought to this chilly response. She was from a vaudeville family and knew that Will's mind was always on the next act. She pulled back the curtain, calling, "Oh, yoo hoo! Ruby! Do you have a moment? You're so clever with the scissors. Could you trim a few of my curls?" She lifted a batch of thick curls as if to demonstrate the problem.

"Of course." Ruby turned back to the orchestra pit. "Thanks, boys! I gotta get a wiggle on."

Just then, the hometown audience began filling the lobby with shouts and high-pitched laughter. As the usher, in a navy-blue uniform with gold epaulets and buttons, showed patrons to their seats, Ruby ran down the stairs and to the chorines' dressing room. Someone had recently posted a hand-written sign on the door.

NO MEN ALLOWED

Laughing, she inhaled the familiar scent of vanilla, greasepaint, and a touch of perspiration as she opened the door. Dressed in their sheer undergarments, the chorus girls were chattering excitedly about the show. At the far end of the room, one was standing with her leg on a chair, carefully rolling a black fishnet stocking up to her thigh. One girl was fastening a corset; others were applying rouge and lipstick.

Ruby smiled and placed her hands on her hips. "Girls, the sign says No Men Allowed, but I happen to know if Rudolph Valentino was in the house and entered like I just did, you'd be happy to greet him."

Necks craned and laughter rang out.

"Oh, Miss Adams! Handsome men are always welcome! You know that," one of the older chorines shouted, causing many of the girls to giggle.

"Say, you look wonderful, Miss Adams!"

At the back of the room beside the wardrobe rack, Clara raised a purple boa and waved with a theatrical gesture.

"Over here, Butterfly."

As Ruby crossed the room, she noticed a young chorine with her nose deep in a *Photoplay* magazine. On the cover was a picture of Theda Bara, the glamorous vamp of silent film.

Ruby tapped the girl's shoulder. "Honey, don't let Mr. King catch you reading that magazine. The moving pictures are a thorn in his *derriere* right now."

The Rossis and Newsoms and other prominent couples climbing the curving staircase to the balcony complained to an usher about the delay in opening the doors.

"We're drenched. Can't you see? It's unacceptable, really, my good man."

"Imagine, all of us standing there in the storm with our umbrellas wide open, waiting to be zapped by lightning."

Basil was trotting down one of the four aisles that led to the stage. He tucked his timepiece back into his trousers as he ran up the stairs and ducked behind the crimson drape. Herman Gil, the stage manager, wearing a pair of striped trousers, white shirt, vest and natty bowtie, was talking to the stagehands.

"Whatever you do, don't drop the curtain too soon. Remember the rule: Never, ever stop a laugh!" The young men, who looked even younger in their knickers and bowties, shook their heads vigorously.

Downstairs, a young boy hollered, "Half-hour up!" Clara LaVelle went to the costume rack and grabbed the knee-length yellow-sequined dress she wore in her first number.

By seven-forty, Ruby was back in her dressing room. More flowers had arrived; bouquets of gladiolas and chrysanthemums in tall glass vases were lined up beneath the ballet barre like soldiers. Inhaling deeply, she caught the fragrance of Mexican tuberose.

"Mmmm, I wonder who sent those?"

She arched her back in a stretch, then hurried to

her vanity table. Working left to right, she placed her face powder, eye shadow, and lip rouge on the white towel, preparing the makeup for her second number.

She looked at her face in the mirror and applied a smidgen of burnt cork to accentuate the dimple in her chin. Then she considered her silhouette. Something was missing. Ruby opened an old cigar box full of notions and picked out a piece of black satin ribbon, tying it around her neck. Then she unlatched a side lock on the vanity and removed a red rhinestone broach, pinning it onto the ribbon. The effect emphasized her décolletage.

"Hello, Lotsa Papa," she mimed.

⎯⎯⌁⎯⎯

Will King stopped in front of the mirror propped against the wall of the right wing and checked his chin whiskers. They were slightly crooked, and he righted them. On the wall between him and Herman Gil was the fly system, which controlled the curtains and all the backdrops. King swaggered over to his stage manager and whispered, "Have you seen this Gloria Swanson picture, Herman? She disguises herself as a boy and joins a gang." He laughed and slapped Herman on the back. "It didn't work in vaudeville, and it doesn't work in the pictures. A bunch of amateurs!"

As the call boy shouted, "Five minutes up," two male dancers ran up the staircase to the stage level.

⎯⎯⌁⎯⎯

Charles Brennan and his wife stepped over a heating vent on the floor and took their seats in the orchestra section. They had a few moments to peruse the program before the house lights dimmed.

Good shows are not rationed.
Will King Presents: The Will King Follies

- Hermie King's Orchestra
- Pathé News two-minute newsreel, Royal Ascot
- *The German Senator,* a Will King monologue
- *Come on, Spark Plug,* a song-and-dance routine performed by Clara LaVelle and Don Smith and the Chorus
- *Ribbons,* a kaleidoscope of color and improvisational dance
- *The Traveling Salesman*, with Will King as Ikey Lichinsky and Lew Dunbar
- *Lotsa Papa,* a one-act musical comedy with Ruby Adams and a BIG, mysterious surprise Intermission
- *An Argentine Fantasy,* a one-act musical number featuring Mildred Markel and Arthur Belasco and dancers
- *Ikey Surprises the Burglar,* a tragic playlet starring Will King and Lew Dunbar
- *Please Be Good to My Old Pal,* a one-act musical sung by Ruby Adams and Valerie

Noyes
- *Finale extravaganza*, all-girl chorus
- *Hummingbird*, an eight-reel motion picture starring Gloria Swanson

As the music from the pipe organ wound down, Brennan, a handsome, blue-eyed man in his early forties, his large head covered with thick brown hair, placed the program on his lap and whispered to his wife, "Vaudeville sure is changing. Gone are the days when chorus girls opened and closed the show. Now the picture reels have the slots at the beginning and end. And it's that picture with Gloria Swanson where she plays a pickpocket who falls in love with a newspaper man. It's a bunch of malarkey!"

Leonora leaned toward her husband. Her eyes seemed to twinkle as she straightened his tie. "Darling, fewer chorus girls is not always a bad thing. We can leave after Ruby's last number. I really enjoy seeing her perform, and she always wears such beautiful gowns."

A well-dressed male came onstage, the main curtain behind him. "Ladies and gentlemen, 'Please Be Good to My Old Pal' will not be performed tonight. In its place, Ruby Adams will sing 'After You've Gone.'" A whistle came from the audience as some applauded. "Ladies, please remove your hats. And gentlemen enjoy the show."

A moment later, the Pathé News began. In the wings, Herman Gil clutched the dog-eared prompt book to his chest. *The book* contained all the information needed for the production: actors' moves, sound cues, lists of props—everything needed to keep the show moving.

"Places. Curtain!" Herman said urgently. The curtain rose and Will King walked onstage to his theme song, "Toot-Toot-Tootsie!" He quickly noted that every seat was taken. Then he took a dramatic bow and signaled to the orchestra to finish.

"Good evening, my dear friends and falling citizens. My heart fills up with vaccinations to be disabled to come out here before such an intelligence massage of people and have the chance to undress such a large...." Full of malapropisms and mispronunciations the city's many immigrants would appreciate, the monologue went on for two minutes.

Herman turned to Clara and her partner, who were lined up "choo-choo" style, ready to take the stage. Don Smith was a decent tenor, but he was clumsy and known to collide with the scenery and props. Both Clara and Herman kept an eye on him at all times.

"Listen to them out there. What a rush!" Smith said happily. "Are you ready, caboose?"

"I am raring and ready to go. All aboard!" Clara pulled on an imaginary train whistle.

As applause rang out, Will King said, "Thank you" and took another bow.

Sitting in front of the fly system, Basil muttered

to himself, "Show time." He took a deep breath and hoisted the projection screen up into the flies. Then he held the rope steady as he secured the line around the spike in the pin rail. His calloused right hand unhinged the second line set and he carefully lowered the scenic curtain that illustrated a train station.

Herman looked down at the book. "Come on, Spark Plug" was set to run ten minutes. A train whistle blew and a snare drum beat out the sound of a train chugging down a track. "You're on at the count of three," he called. "One-two-three."

The heavy crimson curtain went up and the duo choo-chooed their way onto the stage. Herman took a bicarbonate of soda tablet out of his vest pocket and peered out at the audience, waiting for a response. When applause rang out, he returned the tablet to his pocket and sighed.

"Herman," Will King called. "We got a good house tonight!"

"Yes, sir. We sure do."

"Mazel tov." Will saluted as he trotted down the stairs to his dressing room to change for his next act. Herman took another deep breath and turned the page of the book as he waited for the buxom blonde to shake her tail and exit stage right.

After a quick change of scenery, the curtain went up and the chorus girls, gold and pink ribbons attached to their tutus, entered from opposite sides of the stage. "Ribbons" was set on an empty stage with a simple black-drop curtain. As the girls danced, they held a long baton, which revealed red ribbons that their motions kept swirling in the air.

The ribbon dance, which had originated in China, ran seven minutes. For the most part, the audience enjoyed it, but the swirling ribbons and melodic music caused a handful of men who'd brought flasks filled with bathtub gin to nod off briefly.

Then Will King and Lew Dunbar took the stage. The two had performed dialogues for years; King always played the rube, and Dunbar was always the straight man. "The Traveling Salesman" was a classic vaudeville bit, a collection of old routines eight pages long. Herman knew the act so well, he turned his attention to the next act, which would use "black art" or "stagecraft"—the theater term for magic and illusions. Creating black art on stage required an expert degree of preparation.

At precisely eight forty-five, the curtain fell and the stagehands adeptly changed out the scene. Ruby waited in the wing, shifting her hips back and forth with nervous energy. Sweet Daddy Jack got down on his knees and prepared to crawl behind a heavy black curtain upstage. A few feet in front of the curtain, a two-foot-high black fence, or row, blended into the background. Behind the fence was a stagehand clothed all in black, including a black hood and gloves. When he held a spot-lit object above the fence, it would "magically" appear and vanish on command.

Two women laughed somewhere in the theater as

the lighting technician deftly lit the stage to eliminate any shadows. Ruby tapped a two-four rhythm as she reminded herself, "Hit your mark with sharp movements. Look out at the audience. Sing with spontaneity, and smile!"

As the trumpet rang out, Ruby looked over at Herman, who held up two fingers, then one.

The orchestra leader picked up his baton and aimed it at the clarinetist as the curtain rose and the audience erupted in applause. The spotlight illuminated Ruby, strutting across the stage in her tight, black-sequined dress. A long slit in the skirt gave a peek at her shapely legs.

In a breathless manner, she began singing "Come Back, Sweet Papa." The melody's downward progression created a yearning or longing that the audience always felt.

Suddenly, a big gold ring set with a gemstone appeared behind her. The spotlight moved from Ruby to the ring, then back to Ruby as she looked at the audience. "Oh, my! What should I do?"

"Pick it up," several people yelled.

"Make a wish," someone called out.

Ruby turned, her hips swinging gently to the music, as the spotlight followed. She picked up the gold ring and held it out for all to see, then dramatically stroked it, beckoning the spirit world to help her.

The spotlight dimmed as Sweet Daddy Jack shimmied his three hundred pounds between the curtain and the fence. Swirling smoke rose from the stage and a snare drum rattled as cymbals crashed and the spotlight returned.

Ruby stepped aside just as Sweet Daddy suddenly appeared center stage. The audience was full of titters and shouts. "Oooh....myyyyy!" The tall, large man in a top hat peered at Ruby with eager eyes.

Ruby held the ring out toward the audience and asked in a naughty tone, "What am I to do? I know, let's have some fun."

She rubbed the gold ring and said, "Pretty please, spirit world, bring me a ladder."

Thanks to the stagehand behind the fence, a stepladder quickly appeared. "You just wasted your wish!" someone shouted from the audience.

"Hush now, I know what's to be done," Ruby said, wagging her finger as laughter and encouragement filled the house. Ruby knew that once people laugh, you have to keep them laughing. She positioned the ladder so that she could climb up beside five feet eleven, Sweet Daddy. As she climbed up the second rung of the ladder, she used her other hand to gesture to the audience. Finally, she stood eye to eye with Sweet Daddy Jack.

"There, now," Ruby said, "I can whisper into that large abalone-shaped ear."

The audience roared as music rang out.

Ruby jumped down off the ladder, took hold of Jack's hand, and each took a bow as the curtain fell. "I think we squeezed out the laughs," Ruby whispered.

"You're clever that way," Jack replied.

As the applause continued, Herman decided to give them a curtain call. He signaled Basil, whose eyes never left the stage manager, to raise the curtain again. Basil removed the pin and pulled on the rope that lifted a heavy sandbag, the counterweight used to raise and lower the curtains. On the second curtain call, he noticed a snag in the line. It was just a momentary bump, but he made a note to check it as soon as the show ended.

At nine o'clock, the applause died down, the house lights went up, and Leonora turned to her husband. "What a sight! How big a man do you think he is?"

"Well, I've read she's about five feet tall. I'm sure even I'd look like a giant next to her."

Charles Brennan took his wife's hand and led her onto the Carrara marble floor of the lobby, where a white-jacketed bartender was serving refreshments in a corner, baskets of white chrysanthemums on the shelves behind him. Brennan took two glasses of ginger ale from the man and handed one to his wife, saying, "Here you are, darling. It's not Champagne, but there are bubbles."

The fashionably gowned women of San Francisco had draped their wraps over their shoulders, and Leonora had done the same. The couple looked out at the crowd as they sipped their drinks. There was the woman who owned a little dress shop Leonora liked. There was the man who ran the French cleaners. Charles thought he recognized a few court clerks. He assumed the hubbub around the "bar" was Prohibition, since no one had been able to order a legal drink ever since those idiots in government had passed an amendment to the Constitution, no less, outlawing alcohol except for religious and medical purposes.

"It sure is a mixed crowd tonight," he said. "San Francisco is still a small city, and I like that. Why, I'll bet there are people here from the docks and the suburbs."

"Indeed, but look at the hoi polloi over there," Leonora said, gesturing. "Is there anything you'd like to confess to the city's archbishop?"

Charles laughed as he spotted Mayor Jim Rolph, in a pair of striped pants and cowboy boots, talking to Archbishop Edward Joseph Hanna.

"Well, I guess I should tell him that you and I still dream of drinking a Pisco punch."

Lenora laughed. "I'll bet the archbishop dreams of drinking one, too."

As if on cue, a few of the men surrounding the mayor dipped their hands into their breast pockets, pulled out slim metal flasks, and proceeded to spike their drinks.

"Look, there's Big Alma," said Leonora. "Poor woman. Rich, yes, but...." One of the wealthiest (and, at six feet, tallest) women in San Francisco, thanks to her marriage to sugar king Adolph Spreckels, Alma de Bretteville Spreckels was near the stairway to the balcony. A white Cattleya corsage on her black satin gown. Alma's face was creased with age. Her much older husband had passed away the previous summer of pneumonia, and there were rumors about syphilis being the underlying cause.

Alma lived atop Pacific Heights in a Beaux Arts-style mansion and used her charm and her wealth to rule over a variety of local philanthropic activities, including the temperance movement. One of her projects, a three-quarter-scale version of the Palais de la Légion d'Honneur in Paris, had opened the previous winter in a beautiful setting above the Golden Gate. Tender-hearted Leonora hoped the Palace of the Legion of Honor museum was bringing the poor woman some happiness.

"I don't think you have to worry about Alma. I've heard she's been seeing a young cowboy."

"Is that right? Hmmm."

Her husband noted other powerful people at the Strand that night. The hair on the back of his neck rose when he saw Pete McDonough on the staircase behind Alma Spreckels. He was signaling to someone across the room, like a baseball coach with a runner on first base, Brennan thought, staring curiously. McDonough's business was bail bonds, but everyone knew that was a cover for more lucrative activities, such as bribery, gambling, bootlegging, and prostitution. When Brennan was an assistant district attorney, he'd run into

McDonough and his brother Tom many times. As short in stature as Alma was tall, McDonough was dressed in a dark suit and dark shirt. His face was unusually pale, which gave him an unhealthy look. But then, he'd just gotten out of prison.

Leonora took a sip of ginger ale and nudged her husband playfully. "I enjoyed that magic number, didn't you? Sweet Daddy appearing out of nowhere. He looked like a giant St. Bernard next to a little Chihuahua."

Brennan nodded, his mind was elsewhere.

"I wonder how they do that?" she went on.

"I don't have the faintest idea, darling."

The lights in the lobby flickered, indicating the show would resume in a few minutes.

"Shall we?" Brennan asked as the noise rose and everyone hurried to take their seats.

Once the audience had settled into their clamshell-backed seats, a single down-up strum emanated from a Spanish guitar. Mildred Markel and Arthur Belasco readied themselves for their dance-specialty number, "An Argentine Fantasy."

The scene opened in a rose garden in the American Legation, the audience was to assume, Buenos Aires. Mildred entered from stage left in an off-white lace dress with an asymmetrical hemline. Looking stage right, she exclaimed, "Oh, here comes that handsome man now."

On the other side of the rose garden stood Arthur Belasco, in tight pants and a flowing white shirt, his dark hair slicked back. Stroking his thin mustache, he beckoned Mildred with a corny come-hither look. As the orchestra played an "exotic" two-four rhythm, the pair moved into a lead-and-follow-style tango.

Brennan's mind began to wander. Two months earlier, Pete McDonough had been serving time in the Alameda prison. Brennan had read that President Calvin Coolidge had pardoned McDonough of bootlegging charges, and now he was free to bribe the police force and judges of San Francisco again.

When the number ended, Brennan watched as the stage crew scurried back and forth behind the curtain. The orchestra played a few bars of the up tempo "Toot, Toot, Tootsie!" When the curtain went up and the music died down, the audience saw a bedroom scene. A loud snore came from a Murphy bed. Will King was "asleep" in the Murphy bed.

It was time for the burglar to enter, stage left. Herman Gil raised his hand and cued Lew Dunbar.

The audience began murmuring and chuckling, anticipating what was to come. The bedroom window opened, and a man climbed into the apartment. With exaggerated care, he began opening and closing the dresser drawers, looking for valuables. All of a sudden, Will King sat up in the bed, his nightcap at a rakish angle.

In her dressing room, Ruby sat at her vanity in her silk robe, holding a lipstick. The room was so quiet, she could hear the applause for "Ikey Surprises the Burglar." Such a silly skit, but it convulsed the audience every time. Looking at her reflection, she carefully outlined her lips, then filled in the color. Satisfied, she stood up and stepped into her next costume. She was fastening her dance slipper when the call boy knocked on the door and said, "You're on in five, Miss Adams."

"Thank you,"

Onstage, the Murphy bed collapsed into the wall, revealing not just one but four cannons on the underside of the mattress. "BANG. BANG. BANG. BANG." A flash, a cloud of smoke, and the burglar vanished through a trapdoor on the stage as the audience cheered.

Herman looked up just as Ruby ascended the staircase. She was to enter stage right; Will King was to exit stage left. "Ruby, ready? You're on in three!" he called and turned his attention back to the stage.

Onstage, Will King was uttering his most famous line. "Oy, how I *hate* dat guy!" Laughter and applause as the curtain dropped.

King wanted to take another bow, and he looked over at the stage manager, gesturing to raise the curtain. Herman looked toward the fly system and cued Basil. With a callused thumb and index finger, Basil deftly loosened the knot of the sixth rope and pulled.

Clara LaVelle had been watching the skit from the prompt corner. While the orchestra played she and Ruby exchanged knowing grins. How their boss loved to mug for the audience, their smiles said. Ruby realized she had an extra minute; the scenery curtain would be changed out, and then her music would play. She looked in the mirror for a final check and, applying a little spit to her index finger, tamped down the wave at her forehead. Clara said, "Give 'em hell, girl."

Something caught Ruby's eye. "Heavens!" she muttered.

"Ruby, ready? You're on in two," Herman said as he turned to talk with a couple of chorus girls.

"Just a minute! My dance slipper, it's unfastened," Ruby said as she bent over her shoe.

A chilling gust of air whipped through the backstage area. Tiny bits of sand penetrated the eyes, mouths, and skin of the chorus girls as it sprayed everywhere. The stage curtain moved forward and backward just as the painted-bedroom canvas curtain quivered, flapped, and flew upward. The stage manager's body stiffened.

Basil Knoblock stared at his hands. His thigh was touching the lower pin rail used to tie off the rope, and the rope was slack. He tilted his head, and his eyes opened wide as he realized that the fourth-curtain pulley, the one that had stuck earlier, had broken away.

"Jesus Christ!" Herman yelled. The scene had unfolded in slow-moving images. The sand bag falling as Ruby leaned down to fasten her shoe. The bag slamming to the ground and tearing apart.

Sand flying everywhere. Ruby crushed beneath it as if she were nothing more than an insect.

Herman dropped the book and ran to Ruby. "Help!"

The sandbag had fallen from high above the stage in the fly loft and landed directly on Ruby. Herman felt bile form sickeningly in his stomach. Under all the sand, he could see Ruby's body was twisted to one side. Her long, sinewy neck was bent at an odd angle.

Wiping his sweaty forehead, the stage manager crouched down and brushed the sand from her cheeks. Two stagehands fell to their knees beside him and frantically dug the sand away as chorus girls whimpered and cried. Sweet Daddy, who had just returned from having a smoke in the alley, saw the commotion and lumbered over. "Dear God, please, no...our beautiful Butterfly."

Jack carefully lifted two edges of the sandbag, revealing her still, crumpled body. The last time he had seen her, she was jumping down from the stepladder and taking a series of bows with him, looking radiant. He hurled the sandbag against the back wall of the stage. "Get a blanket!" he cried.

In the orchestra pit, the musicians assumed a heavy prop had fallen. At nine thirty the orchestra played 'After You've Gone' and waited for Ruby to walk onto the stage.

The audience members in the best seats had heard the crash, too. Charles Brennan looked at his wife. "What was that?"

"It sounded like one of the cannons misfired," Leonora whispered.

Brennan looked toward the stage and shook his head. "Or thunder? I think I felt the theater shake."

Ruby heard the voices around her. Some girls were crying, and Jack's beautiful voice was asking, almost sobbing, "Ruby, can you hear me?"

For a moment, Ruby thought she had fallen through the trapdoor on the stage. A searing pain resonated through her body, and every muscle in her body felt frozen. Then she heard the opening bars of "After You've Gone." She had to open her eyes.

Exiting stage left, Will King had been greeted by the wardrobe mistress, who placed a morning coat over his shoulders just as they heard a tremendous crash. They bolted for the passageway, pushing past the props piled against the back wall of the theater to the opposite wing. Will forgot all about the show when he saw a girl's leg sprawled beneath a mound of sand. One hand was outstretched, as if she'd been waving to a friend when the sandbag struck her.

"Ai-ai-ai. No!" King cried as he dropped to his knees on the sand-encrusted stage. A welt was forming on her cheek, and blood was seeping through the sand. King draped the morning coat over her and asked helplessly, "Ruby, can you hear me?" He had to raise his voice over the intro to "After You've Gone."

He touched her forehead; it was cold, but she was breathing. Looking across her to Herman, he tried to suppress his growing sense of panic and keep his voice calm. "She's alive. Herman, stop the show!"

Herman nodded, shocked that he hadn't thought to ask this, as the orchestra repeated the song's intro. Suddenly, the audience began to applaud, encouraging Ruby to come onstage.

Ruby strained to open her eyes. Her mouth tasted like blood, and the images in her mind were confused. All she wanted was to sleep. *Get up. Your music is playing. The audience is waiting.* A pain was rocketing through her stomach, and she knew she couldn't go on, but she tried to push herself up. Looking up at Will, she whispered, "The show... you mustn't disappoint. They're waiting." Her voice trailed off, and her world dissolved into black.

Sweet Daddy Jack seemed a little calmer than the others. "I called the hospital," he told Will. "They're sending an ambulance." Behind him, one of the crew was nailing together a stretcher from two two-by-fours and a backdrop.

The orchestra was doing its best to cover the lapse in the show. Herman hadn't been able to move. Will turned toward his cast and crew and said, "Ruby wants us to finish. Let's pull together for the finale. It's what Ruby would want."

A chorus girl said to Herman, "I can't go on. This is crazy! The theater is hoodoo!"

"Are you mad? Get a grip on yourself. We do what Mr. King says."

"Play the music for the finale," Will ordered.

As Herman rose to signal the orchestra, he noticed Clara LaVelle, propped against the stairway to the dressing rooms, disheveled and crying. "Go! Don't worry about me. I'm bruised, that's all. Help her. Help her!"

Abruptly, the music changed keys and the tempo became upbeat. Some in the audience noticed the odd transition in the music. When the chorines took the stage, the musicians were confused, and their timing was off. Some of the girls tried to high-kick or at least move around the stage, but others just stood there, unable to dance or smile. Finally, the crimson curtain came down and stayed down.

The audience was surprised when Ruby Adams didn't perform her last number. And that had been one strange "Finale Extravaganza" with the chorus girls. Even more curious, the show ended half an hour early, and in a huge break with tradition, the cast of the Will King Follies did not take a curtain call. As the lights came up and the orchestra played what was clearly a goodnight theme, people in the audience looked at one another.

"Is that all?"

"Is it over?"

Leonora turned to her husband. "What happened to Ruby's song? And what was wrong with the dancers? They looked like they were in tears."

"Just a backstage mishap, I hope. Shall we go?"

Brennan stood up and stretched his long legs.

Leading Leonora up the carpeted aisle, he raised a hand and mouthed a hello to someone he knew waiting to see if the Swanson movie would be shown.

As they emerged from the auditorium into the lobby, many were talking about where to dine. Brennan happened to look at the back exit, just in time to see Pete McDonough slipping out the door.

◆

Four

The middle-aged man waited quietly on the porch of a redwood cabin in the town of Princeton-by-the-Sea, twenty-five miles south of San Francisco. It was a simple cabin with an expansive view of the Pacific Ocean.

John J. Davis held a Browning semi-automatic in his hand as he looked out through a clearing of cypress trees. The wind was sweeping in from the west, and his fingers were turning red as he clutched the pistol. The *Malahat*, a five-masted schooner from Vancouver, British Columbia, was a few miles off the coast, awaiting a coded radio transmission from the captain's sister-in-law. Allies on sympathetic vessels let her know the whereabouts of local Coast Guard ships, and she sent the information on to the *Malahat*.

The forecast was for wet, nasty weather, and this would be the last attempt to unload the half-million-dollar cargo destined for Davis' restaurant, Coffee Dan's, before the storm made landfall. When the clouds parted and the winds diminished, Davis wiped the moisture from his face and combed back his thinning dark hair with his fingers. Then he placed the loaded weapon on a table and picked up a pair of binoculars. The sea had been churning and agitated, the wind blowing hard, but now the cypress and redwood trees were still.

"The yellow flag just hoisted," Davis yelled. Fifty yards west of the cabin, Davis' procurement boss lay on his belly in a patch of ice plant at the very edge of the bluff. When he heard this, Michael McGowan put his hand to his mouth and let go three sharp whistles. Then he scrambled down a muddy trail, picking his way through the brush.

On the beach, several men in heavy boots and black slickers were dragging three boats equipped with small, powerful engines into the foaming surf. It didn't take long for them to reach the *Malahat* and load a shipment of rum, whiskey, and wine onto their boats. Forty-five minutes later, the men were back on the beach.

At the cabin, Davis was pacing impatiently. To the public, he was Coffee Dan, after the riotous restaurant he owned, in a cellar at Powell and O'Farrell Streets. He embraced the confusion, saying, "Name awareness is key in the restaurant business." Daniel Davis, who opened the original Coffee Dan's in 1878, had died in 1917, two years

before the Volstead Act, which banned the sale of
liquor. His son quickly turned the restaurant into a
"ham-and-egger," which everyone knew referred to
a speakeasy. People said Davis sold more ham and
eggs than anyone. At Coffee Dan's, you could
always count on finding great jazz, hilarious
comedy, and a waiter with a
flask of good Canadian
liquor.

A few large drops of rain
fell just as the *Malahat*
hoisted anchor. The men on
the beach grabbed the heavy
burlap bags filled with
twelve bottles each and
slogged up the trail to the
cabin. McGowan signaled
the men to load half the
bags in a waiting canvas-
covered truck and to store the rest in the cabin.
"Hurry," he said. "Walk quickly and don't break
any of those bottles."

Davis looked up to the night sky. The conditions
weren't perfect, but the night was a success. The
liquor would last at least three months. "Michael,"
Davis called. "I need to get back to the city. I'm
picking up Ruby in an hour."

McGowan shook his head. Davis was almost
twenty years older than Ruby, but he had courted
her for years, and it was clear that he was
hopelessly in love.

———~~~———

As the movie began in the theater upstairs, Ruby lay unconscious in her dressing room, her face badly swollen, her cheeks smudged with dirt and blood. Cast and crew members prayed in the hallway, amid the steam pipes and props. When the door to the dressing room burst open, Will, Herman, and a few others moved aside as Walter escorted a doctor and his assistant into the room.

The doctor quickly completed his examination and said, "We need to move her now!" Covering Ruby with a wool army-surplus blanket and lashing her to a stretcher, he looked at his assistant and whispered, "Unless we hurry, we could lose her."

As the door to the dressing room opened again, someone hollered, "Clear the way." The men carrying the stretcher behind Walter walked upstairs carefully, making sure they did not jostle Ruby. When Walter opened the stage door, a cold gust of wind carried down the passageway.

Bill Finck remained backstage, eyeing the burlap bag. His expression was grave. Someone coughed, and he turned around. Pete McDonough was looking at the sandbag Jack had thrown against the wall. "Bill, I'm thinking you and I should get rid of that. It could cause a problem down the road."

"You might be right," Finck said.

McDonough squinted at the theater manager. "I'm always right."

Officer Patrick Minna, the beat cop, slogged down the Market Street sidewalk, a slicker covering his uniform. It was taking all his energy to hide the fact that he was bored to tears. With this weather, he was anxious to call it a night and join his pals at a speakeasy down the street. He had rousted a few bums from under the window of a nearby pool hall, but that had been it for excitement until the ambulance pulled up at the Strand. Now, pausing at the curb, he watched as it turned onto Sixth Street, heading for St. Francis Emergency Hospital.

Down the cobblestone alley, under the dim light of the gooseneck lamp at the stage door, he saw a group of young men, faces glowing with excitement and curiosity, waiting for the showgirls to exit the theater. Minna had just taken a few steps down Sixth Street when he heard someone calling for him.

"Officer!" It was Walter, the stage-door attendant.

On the other side of the city, Morris Markowitz, president of the New York & San Francisco Amusement Company, which owned and operated the Strand, was asleep. He had made his mark in the film-exchange business—one of the first men to ship movies to theaters on the Pacific coast. Always looking for the next new thing in the entertainment business, he had made and lost a lot of money in his forty-two years.

Downstairs in his new three-bedroom home, the telephone bell cried out from the foyer. Morris' wife tossed the warm green blankets from the bed and grabbed her flannel robe. She felt a chill as she tiptoed down the stairway and picked up the phone.

"Hello?.... No, I'm sorry, he's asleep.... But...."

"Juliette, who is it?" Morris asked from the top of the stairs.

"Someone from the theater."

Alarmed, Morris padded down the stairs and snatched the telephone from Juliette's hand.

"This is Markowitz." He spoke in a low, raspy voice with a slight Romanian accent. After a moment, he sighed. "Where?... What?" He moved the receiver to his other ear. "What's that? Was anyone hurt?"

Trying to overhear what had happened. Juliette stared out a leaded-glass window. Sea Cliff had once been a sandy wasteland at the far reaches of the city. Now stately homes dotted the cliffs overlooking the Golden Gate, but there were no trees or natural barriers to protect them from the elements. The wind blew the rain horizontally, and the two young sycamore trees she had planted in the front yard were snapping like flags.

Morris cleared his throat. "What? Um.... Shouldn't we...? Is there anything I should do?.... I see.... Good night."

Juliette moved toward her husband. "Darling, what was that about?"

Morris was standing motionless by the phone, his blue eyes downcast.

"Morris?" she implored.

"Um...yes?" he asked, shaking his head. "There was an accident at the theater. One of the stars, Ruby Adams, was injured."

"Oh, my goodness! Is she all right?"

"They don't know. She's been rushed to the hospital. They say it doesn't look good," he added, sounding dazed.

Juliette bit her lower lip. "Shouldn't you go down there?"

"What? No, Bill says they've taken care of everything and I needn't worry." Morris sighed deeply and reached out to his wife.

Worried, she held his cold hands. "Can I brew you a cup of tea or...?" Morris was more than upset. He looked uneasy, even fearful.

"No! Thank you."

Bill Finck was Moe Lesser's man. Morris had never trusted him, always felt he was up to no good. He'd heard that Finck was a gambler, and Pete McDonough's goons were around the theater often enough, probably trying to collect. Somewhere in the last year or two, Morris had lost control of the theater's day-to-day operations, and the people in charge now, he felt, were playing a dangerous game.

—⁓—

By midnight, the rain was moving eastward, soon dropping three feet of snow in the Sierra. The coast was crystal clear as the *Malahat* slowly passed the Farallon Islands and headed northwest.

When Davis arrived at the hospital, Ruby lay in the new, modern operating room. Her brother and sisters were already there. The doctors gave him a thorough account of her injuries. "Numerous lacerations, severe concussion, broken ribs—the worst is a crushed spinal column. She may not make it through the night."

"Save her," he cried. "She's young. You've got to save her. And don't spare any expense!"

"Pray for a miracle," they told him.

Unnerved, Davis found the hospital chapel and made his way down the nave. He knelt in the first pew and closed his eyes, trying to imagine what life would be like without Ruby. She was so young and beautiful, so full of joy and laughter—she was everything to him. Davis did not pray long. Gradually, his eyes grew heavy and he fell asleep, the statues of Catholic saints peering out at him from behind the chapel's iron grillwork.

His dreams were of Ruby. She'd been full of life as she'd lounged on a settee in his hotel suite one night, flirting with the idea of moving to Hollywood.

"Listen to this," she said, reading from that week's issue of *Variety* magazine. "'Music halls in London are playing everything but vaudeville acts.

With the falling off of the vaudeville boom, actors are turning to the cinema, which offers steady work fifty-two weeks of the year.'"

"Darling, the audiences are changing," Davis had pointed out. "People are interested in other forms of entertainment. There's not much you can do about it. We need to adapt, love. I'd wager that the ticket receipts of the Pantages, the Golden Gate, or the Warfield surpass those of the Columbia or any other 'legitimate' theater on any given night."

Ruby had nodded thoughtfully.

"Give 'em what they want. Isn't that what they say?" he asked. "I see theater owners in the restaurant night after night, scheming to lock up exclusives with the studios."

Ruby had prodded the dimple in her chin. He knew she was considering Jesse Lasky's offer to appear in two comedies, the first set to begin filming in March. She looked back at John and said, "Let's do it! Let's move to Hollywood!"

———

In the operating room, the anesthesiologist removed the ethylene-oxygen mask from Ruby's face. As Ruby's eyelashes flickered and her eyes slowly opened, Dr. Lennon leaned over the surgical table and whispered, "Smile, Ruby, and we'll let you live."

In the chapel, Davis heard a match ignite. A nun in a white habit, her rosary beads hanging from her waist, lit two votive candles. Davis watched her make the sign of the cross and pray over the candles as he ran his fingers through his hair.

"Mr. Davis, we have been looking for you," she said. "Miss Adams is out of surgery. She's been moved to Intensive Care."

Several days later, Ruby opened her eyes and looked into the anxious face of John Davis. "It's a pleasure to see you again, Miss Adams." His warm hand grasped Ruby's.

"Where have you been?"

"Just left of heaven and two steps..."she whispered.

"Hold onto me I'm staying with you."

A smile of understanding lit her wan face as she relapsed into unconsciousness. Ruby knew from that fleeting exchange that she would cheat death.

◆

Five

Two days later, January's rainfall stood at nine-point-five inches, exceeding the total rainfall of the previous year. The severe rains had destroyed a large swath of the streetcar tracks along the northern tip of the San Francisco peninsula, where the cliffs met the sea. Streetcars were being rerouted from the scenic route along the coast through the city streets.

Early that morning, Charles Brennan sat ensconced in his office in the Humboldt Bank Building, on Market Street across from the Strand about a block closer to the bay. The top of the 1908 Beaux Arts building was a fancy red-domed tower intended to mimic that of the Call Building, on the corner. Inside, a highly ornamented entryway flanked the bank, which promised to safeguard San Franciscans' money in its oversized vault.

It was a slow morning, and Brennan was resting his feet on a box of old case files, sipping a second cup of coffee as he caught up on the weekend newspapers.

San Francisco Call Bulletin

Encores Ended for S.F. Actress, Back Broken by Fall of Stage Sand Bag

Ruby Adams Injured During Saturday Show at Strand

Will King and his Strand Theater Company tried to blithefully sing and crack comedy lines at the Saturday night performance, while Ruby Adams, one of the principal singers and a favorite with local audiences, lay on the operating table at St. Francis Emergency Hospital, her back broken in three places. She had been taken there from the theater after a 300lb sandbag had fallen 20 feet, striking her on the small of her back.

The audience was unconscious of the accident, which occurred while Will King and Lew Dunbar finished their second act. Ruby was awaiting her cue to step on the stage. Suddenly, there came a snap, and a huge bag came hurtling through the air.

The bag struck Ruby in the small of the back, taking her to the floor.

Herman Gil, stage manager, was within a foot of Ruby at the time. Chorus girls screamed. One girl quieted them in time to go before the audience—with artificial smiles on their face.

"Good lord, those dancers weren't cracking comedy lines. The finale was listless! Newspapers," he groaned. "They always print a story the way they want."

Charles Henry Brennan had been the first in his family to graduate from college, later earning his law degree from Boalt Hall, at the University of California at Berkeley. He had started his career in the San Francisco district attorney's office, but after five years of dealing with the city's political machine, its corruption and backroom deals, he left and opened a general law practice with a partner, Harold Faulkner.

Pete McDonough was one of the reasons Brennan left the D.A.'s office. Brennan's boss, San Francisco District Attorney Charles Fickert, had been accused of conspiring with McDonough and two judges to make sure wealthy defendants never faced sentencing. The allegations were never proven, which only seemed to prove the point.

Carrie, his longtime secretary, her blonde hair neatly styled in a marcel wave, poked her head into his office. "Mr. Brennan, you're here?"

"I am. You're brave to come in on such a stormy morning, Carrie."

"Nonsense," she said. "Harold dropped me off on his way to court." She went back into the outer office and was hanging her raincoat on the coat rack when the telephone bell rang. She wiped her hands on her gray wool skirt and picked up the phone, then buzzed Brennan's office. "Mr.

Brennan, the gentleman who owns Coffee Dan's is on the line."

"Coffee Dan's the speakeasy?"

"Yes, he wants to talk with you about Ruby Adams, the actress who was injured at the Strand the other night."

"Funny, I was just reading about that. You know, Leonora and I were at the theater that night."

"Really? That was tragic."

Brennan nodded and said, "Send him through." He quickly grabbed a pen and a pad of paper.

"Mr. Brennan, this is John Davis; thank you for taking my call. Listen, I've been talking to a few friends. I guess you know Paul Updike in the D.A.'s office pretty well. He says you're good at getting around the political machinery in the office and have good relations with the press."

"I have some experience with the press, and I was in the district attorney's office for five years."

"Have you been reading about Ruby Adams' accident?"

"Yes. I just read about it in the *Call*."

"Ruby's my fiancée. The kid's still unconscious, but I'd like to discuss a potential lawsuit against the theater."

The little Brennan had read about the accident suggested it could be a nice high-profile personal-injury case. He needed something he could sink his teeth into. His greatest professional triumph was three years ago. That had been a big case: Brennan had been chief counsel for Roscoe "Fatty"

Arbuckle, the famed silent-screen comedian accused of the murder of a young actress in the St. Francis Hotel.

In 1921, Arbuckle had invited two friends to drive up the coast in his new twenty-five-thousand-dollar Pierce-Arrow to celebrate signing a three-picture contract that would pay him the unheard-of sum of one million dollars. The Labor Day weekend ended with Arbuckle sitting in Cell No. 12 at the San Francisco Hall of Justice, accused of rape and first-degree murder.

Newspapers and tabloids went wild describing the lurid details, true or not, and vilifying Arbuckle day after day. Well acquainted with San Francisco courts and local media, Brennan had been contacted by a group of attorneys in Los Angeles. Two trials for manslaughter had ended in hung juries, and a third acquitted Arbuckle of all charges—the jury had even offered him an apology—but Arbuckle's career was ruined.

Yes, a case with notoriety would be good for his career.

"Carrie," he said, walking into the outer office. "I need you to do some digging on the Strand Theater—you know, who owns what, that kinda thing. Oh, and see if anyone filed a police report on the night of January 10th."

"Yes, sir."

An hour later, Carrie squeezed past the boxes in Brennan's cluttered office and handed him several typed pages. "I have many fears, Mr. Brennan, and one of them is that I trip over all these boxes and break my leg, or worse. Please let me clean your office," she begged.

"No, no...I'll clean it up tomorrow, I promise."

"Right," Carrie sighed, dramatically skirting a few boxes as she left the room.

Her notes revealed that the Spreckels family had built the theater in 1910 and named it the *Empress*. Brennan knew the family owned much of the land on Market Street, leasing the properties to a variety of shops and offices, but this was a surprise. One of the wealthiest families on the West Coast, the Spreckels, needless to say, were very influential people, with close ties to the city's political machine.

Seven years later, the seven-hundred-and twenty-five-seat theater had been sold to Sid Grauman, the theater tycoon, who reconfigured it to accommodate moving pictures and renamed it the Strand. Brennan had run into him during one of Arbuckle's retrials. Grauman had actually discovered Arbuckle, singing in a restaurant in San Jose. Yet once he was arrested, Grauman was the first to cancel all showings of the comedian's films in his theaters. Many assumed that Grauman must know the truth, and other theaters followed suit. Of course, he knew nothing, because he wouldn't return Arbuckle's phone calls.

Grauman had sold the theater to the New York & San Francisco Amusement Company in 1918. According to the city directory, Morris Markowitz

WAITING IN THE WINGS

was president of the company and Moses Lesser was its secretary-treasurer.

Brennan pondered the names and shook his head; they meant nothing to him. Then he began to scribble some notes, at some point writing "responsible party" and underlining the phrase.

"Carrie!" he called from his office.

"Yes, sir?" said Carrie, hurrying in with her notepad.

"See what you can find out about a Morris Markowitz and a Moses Lesser. Then check with the State Compensation Insurance Fund about any safety issues at the Strand Theater. And find out whether there are any lawsuits pending against the New York & San Francisco Amusement Company or either Markowitz or Lesser."

———

Haunting music reverberated from the stopped-wood tibia pipes as the theater organist practiced for the next matinee. Entering his partner's office, on the fourth floor of the Strand building, Morris slowly closed the door and waited for the organist to stop playing. The office, with its metal storage cabinets and wooden crates full of theater tickets, had once served as the nerve center for Sid Grauman and his showman father as they built their theater empire.

"I've been thinking," Markowitz said. "There's a good chance we are going to be sued. Don't you think we should get an attorney?"

Lesser lifted his green eyeshade and looked up at him as if he were intruding on a private matter.

Morris avoided Lesser's cold eyes by staring at a canvas painting of St. Petersburg, which the Russians were now calling Leningrad, on the wall beside him.

"No need to get your dander up," Lesser said dismissively. "I can call my father's attorney and discuss the matter." He had fair Russian skin and a high forehead, but his other features—fishlike eyes, thin lips, and very small teeth—always made Morris think of a carp, or was it a catfish?

"What did you do with the sandbag, Moe?" Markowitz asked. Lesser was making him so nervous, he walked over to the window.

"We thought it was best to get rid of it."

"Really? No one told me."

"I told Bill to relay the message, must have been a slipup. As luck would have it, McDonough was in the theater that night, and Bill asked him to get rid of the bag."

Markowitz raised his eyebrows.

The fact that his father once procured meats for the czar gave Lesser a certain standing among the Eastern European Jews forced to seek refuge from the anti-Semitism pervasive in Europe and Russia. At thirty-two, Lesser had lived in the United States for twenty years, another reason for his arrogance.

Their relationship had begun seven years earlier. Sid Grauman and his father had built theaters in

San Francisco and San Jose, but by 1918, they'd relocated to Los Angeles and were building their Million Dollar Theatre downtown. It would set the standard for the movie exhibitor's art; but the art didn't come cheap, and the Strand could provide needed funds. Markowitz had hoped to purchase the theater himself, but when he heard the price, he went looking for investors.

Maurice Asher was the son of a gold miner who'd struck a vein in the Yukon Territory. His father had insisted he study banking so the family fortune would be well taken care of. Since a career in the city's financial markets provided access to unlimited information, Asher wasn't surprised when Morris Markowitz stepped into his office at the London-Paris National Bank of San Francisco. Markowitz was interested in purchasing the Strand. Within weeks, Asher and Markowitz formed a business in which each man owned two hundred thousand shares.

In a city where just ten percent of the population was Jewish, the Jewish community had close ties. The Ashers and Lessers were members of Congregation Sherith Israel, on California Street, and Asher had done business with the brash young Moses Michael Lesser, helping him sell a theater in the Central Valley town of Lodi. Asher expressed a desire to incorporate in California and that required a board of directors. A third member was needed to prevent tie votes. Moe Lesser was the son of a prosperous man and could get money immediately. Asher and Markowitz issued him a qualifying share in the New York & San Francisco Amusement Company, a decision that led to a serious, long-term problem.

"Morris? Maybe it's time to consider selling the Strand. Get our money out while we can."

"It's not a good time."

The door to the office creaked opened, and Bill Finck poked his head in. He was a short, pock-marked man with sharp features and a heavily waxed mustache. "Boss, I'm going to clock out for about an hour. You need anything?" he asked, ignoring Markowitz.

"Did you finish counting the receipts from last week?"

"They're safe in the safe," he said with a chuckle. "Not that we'll report more than a quarter to the IRS."

Markowitz's close-set eyes narrowed. "You don't want to draw the government's attention," he said in a low voice, "especially now."

"We know what we're doing," Lesser said. "Thanks, Bill. I'll see you later."

Lesser waited for the door to close before turning to Markowitz. "Now, why isn't this a good time?"

"You know Juliette and I are leaving for Paris next week. We're taking the train to New York in a few days."

Lesser mulled this over as he flipped through a

copy of The *Film Daily*. "What ship are you sailing on?"

"The White Star's *Olympic*. Why?"

"I thought I read something.... Let me see. Yes, here it is. 'Before sailing across the Atlantic, Carl Laemmle is wrapping up the distribution deal for *Phantom of the Opera*, starring Lon Chaney, set to release at the end of the year.'"

Lesser looked at Markowitz. "Do me a favor— try to meet Laemmle while you're in Europe. Maybe you'll even be on the same ship. Float the idea and see if there's interest in buying the theater."

Morris sat silently absorbing the request. The four cups of coffee he'd had that morning made his mind race. In 1910, he'd started the California Film Exchange, in a small office in the Phelan Building, with two hundred dollars. When business outgrew the office, he moved to a two-story building on Golden Gate Avenue. It had a driveway, rare in San Francisco, which enabled men to load the movie reels directly into the trucks that sped off to towns and cities up and down the coast.

The company's reputation as the biggest and best-conducted distribution outfit on the West Coast caught the attention of Carl Laemmle, who had merged his motion picture company with several others and become president of the Universal Film Manufacturing Company. Universal, like many pioneering studios, had been based in Fort Lee, New Jersey, until moving west in 1915, the same year Laemmle had purchased

California Film Exchange for a tidy sum, making Morris a wealthy man.

Morris hadn't been ready to retire, however, and he'd stayed on as general manager of the film exchange for the next three years. Morris liked Laemmle's straight-talking manner and admired his gumption for awarding himself the extraordinary salary of a hundred thousand dollars a year. Laemmle immersed himself in details and insisted on daily accounts of the business. Morris wasn't interested in details. While he liked Uncle Carl, as everyone called him, he wasn't ready to deal with him again. He longed for the days when he'd been his own boss and an entrepreneur.

"I'll see what I can do," he sighed. "Can I take that?" pointing to the trade publication.

Back in his own office, Morris removed a cigarette from a gold case, tapped and lit it, and looked through the magazine. There was an article about the admission tax, and another warning theaters that the government could audit their books at any time. He wondered if Lesser had read those articles. His partner tended to cut corners. He had a special relationship with the city's building-permit department, and when he couldn't avoid rebuilding or repairing something in the theater, he tended to put off paying the contractors and workmen. He was putting the company at risk with his lust for profits. Now he and Finck were neglecting to disclose income to the IRS.

Morris walked over to the window and peered down the block to Loew's Warfield, where someone was changing out the marquee. *The Centaurs*, the sign announced, An Animated Fantasy. He cringed as he thought about losing the exclusive contract for this film to the Warfield. The Strand, his baby, had once been a jewel of the theater district, but now she was tired and neglected. He really couldn't blame Marcus Loew for cancelling his contract with the Strand, which had led to the decision to sign Will King's Follies.

Even so, it had been a sweet deal. Will King delivered. He always had a good show, and this one featured a San Francisco darling. People came from as far away as San Mateo to see Ruby Adams.

But Morris had posters advertising moving pictures on his wall, not photographs of fading vaudevillians. He studied the display of meticulously arranged colorized posters. When the Strand had shown *The Navigator* last year, Markowitz had paid for exclusive distribution rights. Buster Keaton was brilliant, and the theater had made a lot of money on that movie.

Not so with *Dream Street*. Markowitz wondered why he still had the poster up. He had thought he'd made a brilliant move with that one. In 1921, D.W. Griffith had been considered the most innovative director in Hollywood. He was extremely ambitious when it came to his craft, and had had tremendous commercial success with *The Birth of a*

Nation in 1915, and *Intolerance,* just one year later. Smaller pictures that followed, which introduced Lillian Gish and Mary Pickford to the public, were also successful. Morris knew that Louis B. Mayer had made half a million dollars from the New England distribution rights for *Birth of a Nation,* and he'd hoped to do the same with Griffith's latest. Markowitz had invested the largest sum ever for exclusive San Francisco distribution rights.

But *Dream Street* turned out to be a box-office nightmare. A romantic "dramatic comedy" set in London, it was big on symbolism, each character representing an aspect of the psyche. Making use of a sound-on-disc process called Photokinema, it even had two short sound sequences. How had it failed, he thought. But the audience stayed away in droves.

And then Maurice Asher died suddenly of a heart attack. Asher knew everyone in San Francisco and New York; he could always secure funding through his friends in the financial markets. Once he was gone, his associates were not as interested in the company. His death forced Morris to bring in a bookkeeper to review the general ledger and cashbook.

"The theater is losing money," the bookkeeper announced. "The company isn't profitable, and there's a total loss of fifty-eight thousand dollars."

"What? Surely it's not as bad as all that?"

"Oh, it is. If this trend continues, you won't be

able to make payroll," the bookkeeper replied, as calmly as if they were discussing lunch. "The loss appears to be due to this film here." He pointed to an entry marked *Dream Street*. "But there's also a shortfall in the cashbooks, somewhere north of ten grand."

Morris was silent.

"Are you aware of this?" the bookkeeper asked.

Morris swallowed. "Well, I may have taken some cash out for travel and entertainment."

He spent the remainder of the year seeking financing from bankers around the country. Many were skeptical of an independent film exhibitor, especially when articles in publications like *Variety* were highlighting the problems.

It's an old story. And an old laugh. That you hear of anything in this business but "million-dollar" pictures. Those that have made that much in 1922 can be counted on the fingers of one hand. There's too much being spent on story material. Too much for names—that mean too little at the box office. Too much for overhead. Too much for everything entering into production. With the result that the average "big" picture has an average negative cost of $150,000 before it gets going. Then add 35 percent distribution and the cost of prints, the advertising, and the interest on the investment before it pays something like $300,000."

Moe had offered to put more money into the

corporation—enough to assume a controlling interest—and wanted to be named secretary-treasurer. Markowitz had felt Lesser was an astute businessman at least, only to learn he was something quite different.

Turning away from the movie posters, Morris picked up a fountain pen and began composing a cable to Carl Laemmle, using deep red ink.

◆

Six

Over the next week, Brennan cleared his caseload so that he could begin work on the Adams case. She was still too weak to receive visitors other than family, and her doctors refused to provide an update on her condition. He waited impatiently to hear from John Davis again; finally, Brennan's telephone rang. "Ruby's awake and able to meet," Davis told him.

"I was beginning to think you weren't coming," Davis said at the hospital, as the iron accordion door of the elevator opened and Brennan, in a gray three-piece suit with contrasting stripes, got out.

"Sorry for the delay. I was held up in court."

They moved past the nurses and nuns hovering over charts at the nurses' station. At six feet, Brennan towered over the much shorter Davis.

"How is she?"

"She has good days and bad days." Davis paused. "I shouldn't kid you, her days are mostly bad."

He escorted Brennan into a private room filled with bouquets and flower arrangements, gifts and get-well cards. The radiator in the corner was making a loud hissing sound.

Brennan glanced at the figure lying stiffly in bed under a mound of bright white sheets and blankets. Her face was just as white. Her hooded eyes, once a stunning feature, looked sunken; her dark hair lay limp against her forehead. She bore little resemblance to the woman Brennan had seen perform "Lotsa Papa" less than two weeks earlier. He positioned himself by the windows in an effort to keep out of the way.

"Darling, I'm back." Davis eased himself toward the bed and kissed her forehead. "How is the pain?"

"Still a lot of pain," she responded wanly.

As they talked, Brennan counted at least a dozen vases. Violets, daffodils, roses, gardenias, and an exotic Ikebana arrangement graced the room. Miniature dolls, including one dressed as a boxer and another as a golfer, sat on a window ledge; a ukulele and castanets were stacked in a corner.

Davis motioned to Brennan to step forward. "This is Charles Brennan, Ruby, an attorney. He was recommended by our friends at City Hall."

She regarded him wearily and said, "Your friends at City Hall, darling."

Davis laughed and rubbed his nose nervously. "Well, you're probably right, but still... I've asked him to represent you."

The attorney towered over her bed. "You're a big handsome fella," she said. "John, take care this gent doesn't stumble and fall on top of me."

Brennan smiled. "I can assure you I'm very steady on my feet, Miss Adams."

"Don't be so sure. It's been said that I can make a man go weak in the knees." Though her voice was weak, she delivered the line perfectly, low and sultry.

"I'm inclined to believe you."

Davis brought a chair close to the bed and motioned for Brennan to sit.

"Miss Adams," Brennan began, reaching into his leather briefcase for a pencil and notepad. "I've spoken with Mr. Davis about your case and how my firm might be able to represent you. I believe you have a claim for damages against the owners and operators of the theater, and I want to file a complaint in San Francisco Superior Court on your behalf. The complaint will state the facts that support your civil action and the damages we're seeking." He paused. "To file the complaint, I'll need to obtain an account of what happened."

"I was in the audience that night," he went on more gently. "So I'm familiar with the show. But what I'd like is for you, as best you can, to describe what happened backstage."

"You were there?" she asked.

"I was."

Her eyes slid sideways to look at Davis. "I don't remember much. It happened so quickly. The last thing I remember is waiting in the wing for my cue."

"Waiting...?"

"I was waiting for Will to take another bow. It gave me an extra minute, so I looked in the mirror to see if anything was out of place."

"Tell me what you saw."

She closed her eyes and pictured the theater. She was standing offstage, in the right wing. She looked down and....

"My dance slipper was unfastened. I bent over and then...." She shook her head. "I'm sorry."

Brennan looked over at Davis and back at Ruby. "I understand. You've suffered a terrible shock. Perhaps you'll remember more later."

"Yes."

Brennan stood up. The heat from the radiator was causing him to lose his train of thought. "Did you bring a playbill or a list of the cast?" he asked Davis.

When Davis handed him the light blue program, Brennan recognized the cover. Just then, a nun in a white wimple entered the room. Having attended years of Catholic school, Brennan stood up and bowed his head respectfully. "Sister," he said reverently.

The nun glanced at him and then over at Davis. "Miss Adams needs to rest."

Brennan looked at the hospital bed. Ruby's eyes were closed.

"Yes," he whispered, "of course."

In the corridor, Brennan considered his next move. He needed to calculate the damages. "John, I'll need to know how much money she's earned over the last few years. Can someone provide me with her tax returns?"

"Her brother can help with that. He takes care of her taxes."

"How long will she be in the hospital?"

"The doctors have no idea."

Brennan pushed the button for the elevator. "And...I'll need permission to talk to the hospital about her expenses."

"Of course, I'll arrange that," Davis said. The two shook hands and Davis headed back to Ruby's room.

Brennan's mood was glum as he left the hospital. Standing at the curb as a Ford coupe rolled by, he felt the chill eat through his pant legs. Across the street was a bakery. Its windows were fogged, but he could see some happy-looking people sitting in booths, and a pot of coffee resting on the counter. A freshly baked sweet might lift his spirits.

The bakery was cheery, with aqua green walls and a well-worn pine floor the color of butterscotch. It smelled of nutmeg and cinnamon, vanilla and fresh coffee. Each table was set with a paper doily on which sat a little pitcher of cream and a matching sugar bowl. Somewhere in the back of the shop, a radio played.

"I'll take a cinnamon twist and a cup of coffee, please," he said to the woman behind a glass-topped counter. Brennan took his twist and the coffee and moved past a laughing group at a table up front to a banquette by the window. Taking the playbill from his briefcase, he studied the cast of the Will King Follies, sipping the full-bodied coffee.

Just as he was enjoying the last bite of the sugary twist, a bell affixed above the door rang. When he looked up, a man in his late thirties or early forties, wearing a raincoat over striped trousers and pearl-gray spats, was walking toward him.

"Mr. Brennan? Can I have a word?"

"Do I know you?"

"No, forgive me for interrupting. I'm Herman Gil, the stage manager for Will King. I just stopped by the hospital to visit Ruby, but she was sleeping. I saw you as you left her room and then noticed you in the window here. John Davis mentioned that you were asking about the show, and...well, I was wondering if I could help?"

"Yes, you might. Can I buy you a cup of coffee?"

"Best offer I've had today."

"Something to go with it?"

As he settled into the booth, Brennan noticed the man looked as if he hadn't shaved recently. "Just coffee, please."

Brennan signaled the waitress and then turned to Herman Gil. "I read in the newspaper that you were a few feet from Miss Adams when the sandbag fell."

"Yes, I was."

When the coffee arrived, Herman picked up the pitcher of cream, poured a teaspoon into his cup, and took a careful sip. "Aww, that's good." He took another sip. "Sorry, I haven't been getting much sleep." As Brennan opened the program, he added, "You won't see my name in there. Will believes the cast should get the credit. Don't get me wrong, he's a great fellow to work for."

"I see. Are you still working for him?"

"Yes, for one more week. It's our farewell week!" Brennan frowned. "Yes," Herman repeated, shrugging. "If the show isn't making money, it's gone. Will always lands on his feet, though. I hear he's got a gig writing sketches for a comedy troupe over at the Geary Playhouse."

Brennan looked past Herman Gil toward the door. It was eleven o'clock and people were leaving. He had a lot he wanted to ask him, but the best way to start was with an open-ended question. "Can you tell me what you remember in the moments before the sandbag fell?"

"I remember everything leading up to the accident vividly. It's like everything was happening slowly. I was in the right wing of the theater. Will was performing that traveling salesman skit, so I was more relaxed; I've seen him and Lew do it a thousand times. I remember I was talking with two members of the chorus after I signaled Ruby. I opened the prompt book just as the trombone played a *wah-wah*." Herman swallowed hard and closed his eyes. "And then...."

"And then?" Brennan prompted.

"Then I remember Will wanted to take another curtain call, so I signaled the stagehand to raise the curtain. That's when, out of the corner of my eye, I saw something fall, and the house shook."

Folding his arms on the table, he opened his eyes and said, "The images are frozen in my mind. You know what I mean?"

Brennan nodded.

"I ran to Ruby...but it was...it was too late. She'd been.... She'd been...." His voice trailed off. He brushed some hair from his eyes and made a strange sound, like a seal barking. "All that life, all that spirit, crushed."

The cashier walked over with a pot of coffee and refilled their cups. Herman looked up at her and then around the bakery; someone was washing dishes in the back.

"What happened after the sandbag landed, Mr. Gil?"

"Please, call me Herman. You make me think you are talking to my father! Well, I remember the call boy shrieking and the chorus girls crying. The music just kept repeating. It was chaos. We didn't know what to do. I think we were all trying to help, but we didn't know what to do."

"I understand." Brennan had been taking notes and now he handed Herman the pad and pencil.

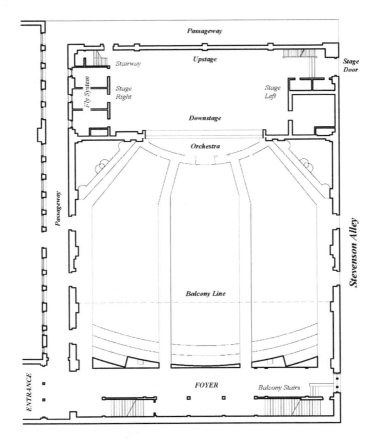

"Would you mind drawing a sketch of the theater's backstage area?"

Gil took the pencil and sketched out a detailed drawing of the backstage, schooling Brennan in theater architecture as he did so.

"The theater has multiple curtains and scenic drops driven by a system of lines, counterweights, and pulleys," he explained. "They call it the fly system. Its basic design is the same as what's used in sailing, only heavy sandbags are used as counterweights to raise or lower the curtains.

"The rope attached to one of the heavier sandbags must have broken apart," he continued. "When I last saw Ruby, the sandbag was on top of her, that and a ton of sand." He inhaled raggedly and started to cry. "I'm afraid my emotions have been getting the best of me."

"Understandable." Brennan paused and pondered the sketch, giving Gil a minute. Finally, he asked, "The paper said it was a three-hundred-pound sandbag, is that correct?"

"Yes, I'd say so. It was one of the larger ones."

After a minute, the stage manager went on, "The theater also has a batch of stage traps for stagecraft effects."

"What is stagecraft?"

"It's when you create an illusion onstage. Magic, a sleight of hand. Mr. King loves it. It's done mostly using stagehands dressed or cloaked in black. They enter the stage through trapdoors or stand behind a black fence that runs across the stage. While the lights are taking the audience's attention elsewhere, poof—something changes upstage."

Brennan picked up the program and slid it across the table. "Which acts used stagecraft?"

Gil looked at the program briefly. "Two. 'Ikey Surprises the Burglar' and 'Lotsa Papa.'"

"Ah, the magic ring."

"Exactly."

There was something about stagecraft that intrigued Brennan. He thought about someone walking around backstage cloaked in black. It was conceivable that something sinister could have happened that night. But why would someone want to hurt Ruby?

Then he recalled how cutthroat people in the entertainment business could be.

"Were there any jealousies among the cast?" Brennan asked.

The question hung between the men for a moment, until the stage manager rubbed his chin. "No, I don't think so. Well, nothing that I was aware of."

By the time Brennan tramped back to his office, the rain had subsided and the clouds had thinned. At the corner of Bush and Battery, in the shadow of the Shell Building, Brennan heard the high-pitched squeal of brakes. He froze on the sidewalk as a truck from the *San Francisco Call* crashed into a vegetable cart. Dozens of tomatoes rolled from the wooden cart along the cobblestone street. One by one, the passersby stopped and stared; several people stood around the cart. As two others helped gather the produce, a dark-clad figure emerged from a doorway, picked up a crate of tomatoes, and ran down New Montgomery. Brennan followed the man with his eyes until he vanished.

Then it occurred to him. "That was a great example of stagecraft."

Once the Humboldt's steel-gated elevator got to the ninth floor, Brennan stood in front of his office, thinking about his next steps. The telephone was ringing endlessly in the insurance office next door. It would be more peaceful inside.

"Good morning, Carrie. Is Harold in?"

"No, he's in court over in Oakland. Something about the factory-accident case you two are working on."

"Listen, see if you can get me a meeting with Will King. I heard this is his last week at the Strand."

◆

Seven

Beauty Stricken
Coffee Dan to wed injured show girl, in hospital
By Ernestine Black, reporter for the Hearst Newspapers

"I'll marry Ruby Adams whether she is a cripple or the light-footed Ruby who danced her way into my heart."

Thus "Coffee Dan," in private life John Davis, admitted his engagement to the girl who was desperately injured when a sand bag fell on her at the Will King show at the Strand Theater, a month ago Saturday night.

Ruby, the girl with the radiant smile, Ruby "the peppiest of the bunch," now lies white and wasted in a room at the St. Francis Hospital.

But there is music in her heart. Not the syncopated screech of the jazz band. The refrain of a love song. The lilt of all the tender melodies of all the ages. Ruby knows that her man is standing by. His final divorce decree is not due for five weeks. Otherwise he would marry her today.

The dream was so real. The saxophone played a syncopated rhythm as she lay next to her lover in an ornate brass bed. Someone called, "Ruby." That was her cue, and she pushed herself to the edge of the bed, but she could not move. A pair of crude leg irons was imprisoning her. Struggling against them, Ruby awoke with a start, her heart beating like a kettledrum. The sleeping pills created some vivid dreams.

Surrounded by the flowers and gifts of her friends and admirers, Ruby no longer dreamed of her future, of dancing and applauding audiences. Her legs would always hold her captive. Not for the first time, her heart broke into tiny pieces.

Sitting up as best she could, Ruby reached for the rectangular metal table next to the bed. On it were seven boxes of chocolates and fudge from a variety of candy shops around town: Blum's, See's, Masky's. She took the box of expensive chocolates from Haas & Sons and looked inside. The pink-tissue-wrapped sweets were dark chocolate almond Fondant Balls, her favorite. She unwrapped one of the candies and placed it in her mouth, which gave her a moment of pleasure. If only she had a cup of hot, rich coffee, she thought.

Looking across the room, she noticed the two folders on the dresser. Inside were her tax returns for the last two years—her past, she thought. Her brother had brought them by for her attorney to pick up. The paperwork did not include the contract she had signed with Famous Players-Lasky, which was appropriate—the contract had represented her future. She wondered if her agent had told the studio she would not be able to honor it.

Down the hall, an elevator rumbled and stopped. The doors slid open and Charles Brennan's large feet hit the floor with force. He was dressed as usual in a three-piece suit and wingtips; his thick brown hair had been cut recently and was kept in place with a small dab of Brilliantine. He had spent the morning in court. Brennan was known as a skilled courtroom lawyer, presenting compelling arguments in a way that held the attention of juries and onlookers. In court, this morning, he argued that his client was not a bootlegger at all, but instead used the five gallons of moonshine to rub down his racing hounds. The Judge wasn't buying it.

A DO NOT DISTURB sign hung from the door of Room 46. Brennan looked at his wristwatch and turned toward the nurses' station.

"Yes, Mr. Brennan, Miss Adams is resting. As a general rule, we are not to disturb patients," the young nurse informed him.

"I understand, but I'm here to pick up papers that are crucial to the legal case I am pursuing on her behalf."

"I understand. Follow me," she said, "but you'll have to be quiet."

As they tiptoed into Ruby's room, Brennan heard the muffled groans of the patient in the next room. A bell rang out, and the nurse looked back to the corridor. "I'll be right back."

Brennan stood in silence next to the window, where the late-morning sun filtered through the blinds. When he inhaled the smell of rich chocolate, his stomach let out a grumble. On the metal table by the bed, with a best-selling crossword puzzle book and a small wicker basket mounded with moss and tiny yellow roses, was an open box of Haas & Sons chocolates. He couldn't help treating himself to one.

On the dresser was a framed photograph of Ruby and two other women. The women all had dark hair and corsages pinned near their décolletage. Brennan had heard Ruby had sisters in San Francisco but had yet to meet them.

When Brennan spotted the folders, he took them to the chair by the window and sat down. One had the words 1923 Income Tax typed on a label across the front. Inside was a three-page form, whose final page indicated a gross income for that year of three thousand two hundred dollars. Three thousand dollars was serious money for a woman to find in her pay envelope, he mused, and very good for an actress. Brennan calculated that Ruby had been making three times more than his secretary. After the war, as the country's economy began climbing a steady path to prosperity, so, apparently, had Ruby.

He removed the short list of employers as he absentmindedly leaned over and took another chocolate. Only two employers were listed for that year: William Morris and Will King. Brennan remembered reading that Ruby had performed in the "legitimate theater," in a drama, and the critics had thought her very good, though she had returned to vaudeville.

In the second folder was an account ledger, with a black tassel to use as a book mark. He took hold of the tassel and opened the ledger to that page. As his fingers guided his eyes through three recent entries, he hummed softly to himself.

Los Angeles:
- $95 for new dress, shoes, and purse
- $25 one night, Alexandria Hotel
- $12 cosmetics

"Mr. Brennan, is that Gershwin you're humming?" Ruby asked groggily.

Brennan hadn't wanted to gaze at Ruby while she was sleeping. Now, when he turned to her, he saw she was slightly elevated, as much as she could be in a body cast. "It is, but please call me Charles."

"I like Gershwin, too," she said, adjusting the tie on her flame-colored bed jacket, her hair held off her face by a beaded headband. "Sometimes his melodies get stuck inside my head for weeks at a time. I knew the two of us would get along. And I see you've found the paperwork," she said. With her black hair and the orange jacket and headband, she made Brennan think of a Monarch butterfly.

"I am impressed with your recordkeeping," he said.

"I try." Ruby cleared her throat. "I'm rude to have fallen asleep before you arrived. What time is it?"

"Eleven-thirty…and the sun has finally granted an appearance."

"Oh!" she said with renewed energy. "Please, open the blinds. I'd hate to miss such an important event."

He twisted the blinds open and sunlight cascaded into the room.

"Oh, my! It's so nice to see that lucky old sun again. How I wish I could jump up and look out the window."

"The view isn't much," Brennan said, peering out, "just a vacant lot with a few eucalyptus and bottlebrush trees. But there are some beautiful white puffy clouds." He paused. "I think I see some butterflies. And it's queer, but just now I was thinking you looked rather like a butterfly."

As he turned his head from the window, he could smell a hint of jasmine.

She smiled at him. "Pardon?"

"A butterfly," he repeated. "Isn't that what some call you?"

Her hands fluttered in front of her as she pointed to the window. "Yes. That's the ticket. I must rise from my chrysalis and fly south."

She envisioned herself standing next to him and

peering out at the sky, the empty lot, the trees and butterflies.

"Oh, hell, I wish I could get up and walk over to that window, but my wings have been clipped." she said. "You know, after the earthquake, I lived with one of my sisters, not far from here on California Street. It was hard to find housing, and even though she had just married, she took me and my sister Mae into her house. I'd borrow my brother-in-law's bicycle and ride it all around the neighborhood, waving at our neighbors. Oh, I was quite the showoff." Her voice trailed off.

"This picture, are these your sisters?"

"Yes. They sacrificed a lot for my career. I don't know what I'd do without them." She told him how, after their father had died and several siblings left the city to find work, her sisters and brother had indulged her drive to learn and better herself. They had scrimped on food at times so that she could take dance lessons, or buy a dress for an audition or a performance, so that she could work toward her dream of performing. They would chaperone her at recitals and pick her up late at night.

She sighed, and Brennan saw in her eyes the yearning for a lost world.

"I'm sure it's what they wanted," he told her.

After a moment, he turned back to the ledger.

"Are these all your expenses?"

"Yes. I assume my expenses will be very different... now."

Brennan imagined that her offstage life had been full of parties, dinners, and travel. Now she would need twenty-four-hour care and have to live on the ground floor of any building that lacked an elevator. Yes, her expenses would be very different now.

"I'll need to look at your contract with Will King," he told her.

"My agent has that. He's with the William Morris agency."

"Good. I'm interested in the terms of your employment."

The moaning next door was getting louder. A bell rang out sharply four times, and they heard people run down the hallway.

"Poor soul lost his wife in a fire, the nurses told me, and he's suffering with third- degree burns."

"Behind each door is a sad story, I'm sure, Miss Adams."

Ruby frowned. "Is that what I am, just another sad story, Mr. Brennan?"

"Of course not. You're my client, Miss Adams."

"I see." She pondered that thought. "Life can change so quickly......"

He looked at her, chagrined, realizing he had hurt her. He wanted to apologize but was embarrassed by his insensitivity.

"Please go on," Ruby requested.

"Why were you in Los Angeles last December?"

"To do a screen test. I was set to leave vaudeville."

"Why?"

"I was going the route of all good vaudevillians—to the dark side." Brennan looked startled, and she grinned. "That's what vaudevillians call the picture shows, the dark side. You know, the moving pictures are all black-and-white, no color."

"I agree, motion pictures aren't as beautiful as live theater, but they have their appeal. I'm sure you would have wowed them."

She noted the verb tense he used and nodded. The screen test at Famous Players-Lasky seemed years ago.

"Two months ago, I was standing in a barn in Hollywood taking a screen test. I wore a bathing suit and held a dead fish under the hot Klieg lights. How's that for glamour?" She laughed.

Brennan tried to smile.

"John, my fiancé, and I were asked to join Jesse Lasky and his wife for dinner at the Cocoanut Grove. We hadn't expected that, and I had to buy a new outfit."

The door opened, and Brennan heard a sudden rustle of packages, carried by two small, dark-haired women who looked very much like Ruby.

"Here they are, sneaking food and cakes past the nurses. Charles, these are my older sisters, Edna and Mae."

Brennan nodded politely and sat quietly as the women greeted each other, laughed and hugged and fussed over Ruby's appearance. It reminded him of his wife's Friday- afternoon bridge games in their home, only more personal. He didn't want to intrude.

He stood up with the folders and bowed slightly. "Ladies, I'll leave you to it."

In the lobby, he spotted a group of reporters and photographers. Brennan considered what he wanted to say and then stepped forward. By now, all the local papers knew he was representing Ruby Adams.

"How's Ruby doing?" one reporter asked.

"Will she be suing Will King? What about the theater?"

"Guys, guys, patience!" Brennan said in his friendly, easygoing way. "Miss Adams is doing as well as can be expected. She's getting a great deal of encouragement and support from her family and friends. She's not strong enough yet to make a statement."

That was the beginning of Brennan's legal strategy. No encouraging words about Ruby's condition. She must appear to be weak, a victim, her future and finances in doubt. Also, he thought, it would be best if she and John Davis did not wed anytime soon.

◆

Eight

A week earlier, Brennan had stood outside the Strand Theater debating his next move. It was almost one o'clock, and he knew the theater wouldn't be open for another hour. He crossed the broad avenue and made his way to Lesser Brothers Market, on the ground floor of the Flood Building. Carrie had learned that the family of one of the officers of the New York & San Francisco Amusement Company owned the market. Lesser Brothers was known for its Russian bread pockets, and Brennan hadn't eaten lunch yet.

Prowling the grocery aisle, he found a middle-aged, blue-smocked clerk stocking shelves.

"Excuse me."

"Hello, may I help you?"

"Any *piroshky* today?"

The woman looked toward the cash register. "The person who can help you must have stepped away. Follow me. How many would you like?"

"Two, please."

Brennan loved the Russian bread pockets, with their savory filling. The woman ducked below the counter and came up holding two piroshkies, which she carefully placed in a brown bag.

"Are you hiding them?" Brennan asked, laughing.

The woman chortled. "Well, they are popular."

"Who makes these delicious piroshkies?"

"I do."

"Oh, are you Russian?" he asked in his friendly way.

"Oh, heavens, no! No Russian blood in these veins," she said, looking at the veins and liver spots on her hands. "I'm Irish. The family that owns the market is Russian. Mr. Lesser taught me how to make them. He's very talented. He procured meats for the Russian royalty!"

"Really? I guess the meat here must be pretty good then."

"Oh, yes, best in town! He moved to America before the Russian revolution. Good thing, I'd say. What I mean is….what they did to the czar and his children was terrible!"

The two eased into conversation, during which Brennan learned that the market sold the best Midwestern beef in the Bay Area. The vegetables came in every morning from the fields in Daly City. There were two sons. One managed the Saratoga Market, the other worked in the theater.

Brennan said, "I think I'm going to pick up a few

steaks before I leave. Thank you for your time."

At the meat counter, a powerfully built man in a white apron smeared with blood was using a large knife to trim the fat from a side of beef. The butcher's eyes narrowed when Brennan asked about Moe Lesser. "Yes, he's with the Strand Theater." Looking around, he added, "You a copper? If so, you should know we do business with the McDonoughs. Most of the shopkeepers around here do business with the McDonoughs."

Pete and Tom McDonough offered many retailers, especially those known to sell liquor, protection from petty theft and the police. Brennan raised his eyebrows, feigning surprise. "Me? No. Just an attorney."

Brennan walked a short distance to Powell Street and the cable-car turnaround. After weeks of inclement weather, San Franciscans were taking advantage of balmy skies. A handful of people milled about, laughing; others were shopping or having their shoes shined, now that the rain had finally cleared.

Brushing off a bench, he sat down in a small patch of sunlight as the cable car approached. Once it stopped and all its passengers disembarked, a group of young revelers whirled it around, scattering a cluster of pigeons. On the opposite side of Powell, an older man sat working in a crossword puzzle book. Brennan closed his eyes and savored the sun on his face. Soon the cable car's grip man rang the bell and the car began ascending the three hundred and seventy-six feet to the crest of Nob Hill.

Tossing the brown bag into a trashcan, Brennan walked quickly across Market to the Strand. The Strand's marquee hung impressively over the curb. *Along Came Ruth*, starring the boisterous Viola Dana, would begin at three o'clock, still an hour away. The movie had been a great success, but it wasn't a new release.

Brennan headed down the narrow pedestrian walkway to the theater entrance. A woman with a baby carriage was peering into a lingerie-shop window; a sign advertising billiards hung over a doorway that led to the second floor. The passageway looked very different without the crowds Brennan was accustomed to. He'd never noticed the sign before. Cigarette butts, broken glass, and gum wrappers covered the ground, and he thought he could smell urine. The place was in need of a thorough cleaning, he thought.

Through the theater's glass-paneled oak doors, he saw a janitor washing the marble floor, a small man in coveralls with a cloth mask around his mouth. When Brennan rapped loudly, the janitor pulled the mask down and shouted, "We don't open for three quarters of an hour!"

"I want to speak to someone about the backstage," Brennan called.

The man dropped his mop, grabbed a ring of keys, and walked to the door. "You the general contractor?" he asked, giving Brennan no time to respond. "Come on in."

As Brennan inhaled the sharp odor of ammonia, the janitor turned and said over his shoulder, "I'll be right back."

The pipe organ was playing a jaunty tune as Brennan looked around the empty lobby, with its gleaming mirrors and sconces and polished brass railings. The mirrors had provided a good view of the crowd the night he and Leonora had been at the Strand. The society folks had been preening, and so were the politicians.

Ten minutes later, the organ stopped, and Brennan sighed impatiently. Finding nothing to discourage him, he crossed the lobby and entered the auditorium. After his eyes adjusted to the dim light, he walked slowly past the soundproofed crying room, where mothers retreated with their children when necessary, and down a center aisle. He was standing halfway down the aisle, next to row H and the seats he and Leonora had occupied the night of the accident, when a man's voice rang out.

"Hello! I'm Jeffrey Asher, the assistant manager. May I help you?"

"Yes, I'm here to take a look at the backstage. Name's Charles Brennan. I'm representing Ruby Adams."

The man looked confused. "What? Dutch said you were the contractor."

"I'm afraid the gentleman didn't give me a

chance to explain myself. But I'm here, so if you don't mind, I'd like to take a look backstage, where the accident happened."

Asher was an affable young man, with a round face that featured impressive dimples. There wasn't anything to see backstage; the sandbag had been removed and a new sandbag hung in its place. "I guess that's no problem. I wasn't in the theater that night, but from what I've heard, a sandbag fell in the right wing. Follow me."

For a large man, Asher practically bounced down the burgundy-colored carpet and up the side stairs to the apron of the stage. "Through here," he said as he drew aside the grand curtain.

The two men walked to their left, which was stage right. Brennan negotiated his large feet through a maze of electrical wires and examined his surroundings. "Would it be possible to turn on some lights?"

Under Asher's watchful eye, Brennan assessed the area as a series of lights flicked on. The backstage was very different from the luxurious public areas. A complex system of ropes and pegs hung from one wall. Old furniture, dusty props, and a discarded wooden crate were scattered willy-nilly in the wing, along with a mismatched pair of dance shoes and a flaxen wig. The distinctive musty smell reminded Brennan of his grandmother's house in the Richmond District.

Ahead of him the stage; behind him, a stairway that led downstairs to, Asher informed him, the dressing rooms. Brennan walked through slowly, the soles of his wingtips crunching on bits of sand. The most interesting piece of evidence was a mirror, propped against a piano. This is where she was standing, Brennan thought with a sick feeling.

Tugging up his trouser legs, he knelt on one knee and examined the planks of wood near the mirror. There was a deep gash in the pine floorboard. Prodding the gash with his index finger, he found tiny granules of sand; clearly, the theater owners hadn't spent any money fixing the floorboards or cleaning up. They don't spend money on the parts of the theater the audience doesn't see, he thought.

"Is it possible to see the ropes and the sandbag?" Brennan asked, looking up at the fly loft, with its myriad of ropes and six more sandbags.

"We replaced everything, of course."

Brennan looked surprised. "I see. Is the original sandbag still here?"

"What? No. I suppose the stage attendant cleaned that up."

"What's his name?" Brennan asked.

"Walter Hall, but he quit a week or so ago."

Brennan pulled out his notepad and scribbled a note to ask Ruby about Hall.

"Well, let me see how the sandbag works."

"Pardon me?"

"I've heard about fly systems, and I'd like to see how this one works."

Asher looked up and contemplated the fly system. "Right."

The two-tiered fly system was impressive. It had two horizontal rows of wooden cleats that tied off the ropes, securing the curtains and scenic drops to a pin rail. Asher spit into his hands and untied the knot holding one of the rope lines.

"The line set runs from a batten above the stage up to a grid. When you pull down on the line, it pulls over the block and lifts the batten," he explained. "It's like a seesaw." He grunted as he pulled hard on one of the lines and the stage curtain began to rise. "The sandbag is used as a counterweight, and the curtain rises," he said, nodding toward a beam in the rafters.

Brennan was silent as he looked up at the fly loft.

"Mr. Brennan, I really shouldn't be doing this. I'm not exactly familiar with the equipment."

"How much weight is in one of those sandbags?" Brennan asked.

"Depends. Sandbags come in all sizes. They can hold twenty-five, fifty, a hundred pounds or more. To increase the weight, you can add a brick." The thought made Brennan shudder.

Walking over to the fly system on the wall, Brennan studied the ropes. "How often is a line raised and lowered during a theatrical performance?"

"Oh, heavens, in a musical show…many times."

Brennan peered at the rafters, past a dozen ropes that led up to the beam. He caught a glimpse of sunlight—a hole in the roof? Was the roof in need of repair, too?

"Who maintains this system?"

"Basil Knoblock is in charge of the fly system, and he makes the inspections."

"Who does he work for?"

"Us."

"Meaning the theater?"

"Yes."

"Does he still work here?"

"Yes."

"How do you spell Basil's last name?" Brennan was writing the name in his notebook when he heard someone approach. He put the pencil behind his ear and waited.

"Jeffrey?" A voice, low and clear, came from the stairway.

"Over here, Mr. Finck!"

"Dutch told me the contractor was here."

A man holding a piece of wood came into view. "What's this all about? You don't look like a contractor." His voice and manner were equally cold.

"This is Mr. Brennan, Ruby Adams' attorney."

"I'm here to get a look at where Miss Adams was injured," Brennan explained.

The man looked surprised. "Jeffrey, did you talk to Mr. Lesser about this?"

"Why, no, he isn't in."

"I'm not sure you should be allowed back here, Mr. Brennan. Too many hazards. Don't get me wrong, we have nothing to hide, but we must talk to the boss."

With his sharp features and ice-cold eyes, not to

mention that villain's mustache, Finck's appearance was as off-putting as his manners. "I understand, but I'm here now, Mr. Finck," Brennan said politely. "This shouldn't take more than a few minutes."

"Let me put in a call into Mr. Lesser. You wait here," he said.

When January had passed without notification of a lawsuit, the officers and staff of the New York & San Francisco Amusement Company had made a collective sigh of relief and continued business as usual. So Finck had been caught off guard. Five minutes later, Brennan wasn't surprised when Finck told him, "Just as I thought, Mr. Lesser ain't in. That means I'm in charge, and you are trespassing."

Finck reached out, took the chewed-up pencil from behind Brennan's ear, and broke it in two. He smiled an unfriendly smile and said, "Nice to meet you, Mr. Brennan. Now, let me show you out."

As Brennan was escorted toward the apron of the stage, he asked as if it had just occurred to him, "Oh, one more thing. Was a police report made of this incident?"

Asher and Finck looked at each other, and Asher shrugged. "I think I heard the beat cop stopped by after the show."

"If I were you, I'd check with the coppers down at Southern station," Finck said.

Leaving the theater, Brennan noticed the fog beginning to crest over Twin Peaks and felt the chill in the air. He inhaled the acrid smell of gasoline leaking from a taxi at the curb as he pondered what he'd learned.

- The sandbag had been discarded. Ask police if they have it.
- Bill Finck, the theater manager, had hardly welcomed Brennan's visit. Breaking the pencil had to be an implied threat.
- Basil Knoblock was working the fly system that night and still works at the Strand.
- The backstage area was terribly neglected.

Directly in front of him, on the sidewalk, was a legless man selling pencils. He was perched atop a piece of wood the width equal to his two legs with rolling casters. His trousers pinned and folded at the knees. Brennan dropped a nickel into the man's tin cup and took a new pencil.

◆

Nine

Brennan paced back and forth in the hallway. Sometimes his office was just too cluttered to think in. It was peaceful in the hall, just the constant click-click-click of a typewriter in the insurance company next door. An accountant in the office had helped Brennan deal with the life-expectancy figures for Ruby's case.

Now he ran his fingers through his thick hair as he reread Ruby's contract with Will King. The contract stated that theirs was an "at will" relationship, whereby "the manager" or the "business" could release "the act" at any time. With all its jokes, songs, parodies, and sketches, a vaudeville show tended to be dependent on stock material—which was stressful on actors who could not improvise. It was clear that if "the act" failed to win over the audience, he or she would quickly be let go.

From Ruby's most recent tax returns, however,

Brennan could see that she'd been in demand. Performing regularly onstage and in cabarets—most often with the Will King Follies, on the Orpheum Circuit—she had worked an average of forty weeks a year. Her performances yielded about three thousand a year, and her testimonials earned her another thousand. The ledger revealed her life on the vaudeville circuit was full of suitcases, trains, and travel, but it paid off, and her income continued to climb. Her pay had increased by nearly thirty percent each year.

In addition, she had received fees from advertisements and endorsement deals with clothiers and hosiery shops. Davis had told him that every three months, one prominent San Francisco dressmaker sent her a new evening gown, which Ruby was to wear to banquets, formal dances, or other society functions at least twice.

And then there was the contract with Famous Players-Lasky. Just a month before the accident, Ruby had committed to making two pictures with the studio over the next year, for a salary of seventy-five dollars a week—good steady money after working in vaudeville for more than a decade. She was to arrive in Hollywood by March 5.

As Brennan mulled over his chicken scratches, he inhaled the aroma of roasting coffee beans from the new brick Hills Bros Coffee plant at the Embarcadero. Just as he turned to the medical expenses Ruby was racking up in the hospital, he noticed that music had replaced the typing.

Someone was listening to a radio. Gershwin.

The door to his office creaked opened. "There you are," Carrie said. "Why are you out here?" she looked bewildered.

"I needed to think. I'm working through the numbers."

"For Miss Adams?"

"Yes. I think I've arrived at a number. I'm going to ask for a hundred thousand dollars."

"Compensation?"

Down the hall, the iron gate of the elevator snapped shut and they could hear the grinding of the elevator shaft.

"You don't agree?" Brennan asked.

"It's not that. It's just—how do you put a price on someone's legs?"

Carrie knew Brennan couldn't really answer the question. She watched him slowly crack the knuckles of his right hand, one by one.

"Your eleven o'clock appointment called and said that he's been delayed. He asked if you could meet him at the Geary Playhouse instead."

Brennan nodded.

"Oh, and don't forget you have a three o'clock in Oakland," Carrie reminded him.

———

It was almost eleven when Brennan stood in front of the 1910 Classical Revival theater, with its tall arched, colonnaded windows above three double doors. One of the first theaters built after the earthquake, the Geary Playhouse sat just across an alley from the much newer Curran Theater, opened just three years earlier. The ornate double doors were labeled Comedy, Geary, and Tragedy. Brennan took the door on the right, Tragedy, and immediately hoped that hadn't been a mistake.

"Mr. Brennan?" someone called as soon as Brennan stepped into the lobby.

A short, stocky man in a brown tweed suit and black-and-brown spats, a watch chain draped across his vest, was standing about a dozen feet away. Out of costume and makeup, Will King looked much older than he had onstage.

"Guilty."

King laughed appreciatively. "A lawyer joke!"

"Only works the first time," Brennan said.

King nodded. "Don't I know that feeling. Come on, let's sit in the auditorium. Follow me."

King briskly ushered Brennan through a leather-covered door and down a narrow aisle. Though they were not much apart in age, Brennan suddenly felt his forty years.

"It's a crying shame what happened to Ruby," King said mournfully as they took two front-row seats and looked up at the stage. Several young stagehands in sweaters, baggy pants, and wool caps were breaking down a set from *Up in Mabel's Room*. It was a play that King knew well; he had created a parody for the Follies. Now Clara LaVelle was appearing as Mabel, and King was a producer.

Brennan remembered that he and Leonora had seen Sarah Bernhardt, the famed French actress, at the Geary Playhouse, playing the lead in *Hamlet*, when Bernhardt was touring the States some ten years earlier. The theater, while a jewel, was small and staid in comparison to the Strand.

"No sense beating around the bush," Brennan said. "Who's responsible for the equipment in the theater?"

King swallowed. He had spent the previous day at the hospital. "Ruby just asked me that question," he said, his eyes fixed on the stagehands. He gave a deep sigh. "My company is in charge of all the props. The theater is responsible for the lights and curtains, the scenic drops—all the fixed equipment. A fella by the name of Basil was controlling the fly system that night."

"Is that standing operating procedure or is it detailed in the contract?"

"It's written into the contract. I pulled it for you." He reached into his breast pocket and pulled out some papers. "It's pretty clear that the New York & San Francisco Amusement Company is responsible for the equipment at the Strand."

Brennan took the four-page contract and quickly scanned it as Will King fidgeted. His Jewish guilt had driven him to pay the fifteen-hundred-dollar bill for the ambulance and emergency-room services, and he was paying sixty-four dollars a month into the Workers Compensation Fund for Ruby. But in the end, it appeared that the New York & San Francisco Amusement Company was responsible for the accident. Paying the hospital bills was one thing. Paying for someone confined to a wheelchair for life was a whole different kettle of fish.

"How familiar are you with the man who signed the contract, this…" Brennan looked down at the bottom of the page, "M.L. Markowitz?"

"Know him? He's the one who sacked us."

"What's that?"

"He sacked us. After the accident, he felt our ticket receipts weren't what they needed to be. That's why I'm working here."

Brennan was silent for a minute. "What kind of man is he?"

"Morris Markowitz has been in the film industry for years." King paused, wondering how to explain what he felt about Markowitz and his ilk. "Vaudeville's an art, Mr. Brennan, a beautiful art— not an industry. Mr. Markowitz has little appreciation for the art and has a one-track mind. He wants to be a big cheese in the movie industry."

"But the man is an independent exhibitor, which means he owns the theater but he doesn't own the films. You'd think the business controlling the customer would have the power, but no. These days, the big studios have ways of controlling the theaters."

"Go on."

"Well, for instance, a couple of years ago,

Paramount Pictures asked the independent exhibitors to sign contracts that were essentially all or nothing: If they wanted the big stars and big pictures, they had to take the studio's smaller pictures, too. Many of the independent exhibitors, I heard, wouldn't sign the contracts. Markowitz signed a deal with Goldwyn-Cosmopolitan, but Marcus Loew bought out the studio last year, and he cancelled the contract with the Strand, because Loew's Warfield Theater was just across the street. Markowitz decided to offer a combination bill—second-run pictures, newsreels, and vaudeville—and that's why we were performing there."

"I'm sure you've noticed the theaters on Market Street are all showing moving pictures now. Paramount started a war buying up local theaters, like the Granada. This Adolph Zukor fellow, the guy who started Paramount, is collecting theaters like postage stamps, and Fox, Loew, and First National have followed suit."

"So the Warfield is owned by Loew's?"

"Yes, but now it's called Metro-Goldwyn-Mayer."

"I see."

"They call it *vertical integration*. What poppycock. The production company produces the film, controls the distribution, and owns the theater. Pretty soon the vaudevillians won't be able to find a theater that'll hire us."

"But surely you'll be able to play alongside the moving pictures, like at the Strand?"

King shook his head. "A vaudeville show puts more wear and tear on the old equipment. The theater owners need to maintain the backstage and equipment, man the stage door. They can make a lot more money just raising the curtain and running the celluloid, and they can show the same pictures again and again. Yes, I think the end of live performance is here."

Brennan considered the statement. The Geary was quiet; the sets were gone and the stagehands had disappeared, but he could feel their presence, their energy. He thought about Bernhardt's performance in *Hamlet*—he and Leonora had agreed it was one of the best evenings they'd ever spent in a theater. Live drama and comedy, even vaudeville, was intimate, while a motion picture, even if entertaining, felt distant and...flat, just as Ruby had said.

"What about this theater?" he asked, gesturing toward the stage and the seats around them.

"It's really nice but small, not many seats. The picture people want the larger theaters. So for now, we are safe."

"It would be a shame to lose live theater," Brennan said. Then, getting back to business, he held up the contract. "I'd like to review this more closely. May I hold onto it?"

"Sure. Keep it."

Brennan opened his briefcase and placed the contract on top of the other papers. He decided to throw out a question. "Is Ruby well liked by the cast?"

King looked puzzled. "That's an odd question."

"I mean, could anyone want to do her harm? You know, jealousies among the cast or crew?"

"No. Absolutely not. We were like family."

"All right. As I understand it, you were leaving the stage at the time of the accident. Could someone have wanted to hurt you?"

King looked at Brennan sharply. "You think this was intentional?"

"Mr. King, as Miss Adams' attorney, I need to investigate all options."

"What makes you believe this might have been an accident?"

"In a civil case, a plaintiff has to prove she was harmed because of someone's acts, either intentional or negligent. I want to explore the possibilities of negligence and sabotage and anything else that might have resulted in Ruby's injury."

"I don't know." King leaned back in his seat. "I can't see the advantage in hurting her, or me. But... you know, some of the cast was glad to leave the Strand after the accident, even though not everyone has gotten work. Theater folks can be superstitious, and some of them are saying the Strand is hoodoo."

"Really? You mean it's haunted, or bad luck? What do you think?"

"I think it's silly. So no, I don't think it is. I hope not."

Brennan rose from his seat and shook his legs to regain circulation, then handed King his card.

"Mr. King, I hope not, too. My office will be contacting you for a deposition in the coming weeks."

◆

Ten

With each passing day, Ruby faded a little more from public consciousness. Fewer flowers and gifts arrived at the hospital; the newspaper articles about her subsided. Doctors with probes had pricked her ankles and feet again and again, although she couldn't feel a thing. She struggled to move her legs, desperate to prove the doctors wrong. "I hate this." Ruby looked up at her doctor and asked, "Is there any hope that I will ever dance again?"

The doctor solemnly shook his head and said gently, "No."

She had asked the question in different ways to different doctors, but the answer was always the same. She abhorred standing still.

"Surely there's a chance that I could walk at least?"

"No. I'm sorry."

"God, what will I do?" she asked the priest who came by weekly to give her communion.

"God believes you have the strength to live with this burden, my child," he replied.

Science and religion had given their verdicts. Ruby's paralyzed legs would never carry her before the footlights again, or anywhere else. If his words were intended to lift her spirits, he failed.

Her nurses did their best to comfort her. The elderly, all-business nurse brought her butterscotch and peppermint candy. She had her lover and her family and, thanks to the sleeping pills, her vivid dreams. Dreams of her mother. Dreams of the earthquake. Dreams of Sophie Tucker and Paul Whiteman—now, after commissioning *Rhapsody in Blue* from George Gershwin, such a famous bandleader. She dreamed she was dancing on the stage at the premiere in New York, with Gershwin at the piano.

"Miss Adams?" came a voice from the doorway. It was one of the young nurses.

"Yes?"

"You have a visitor. Mr. Brennan is here. He has some papers for you to review."

"All right. Can you hand me my bed jacket and a mirror?"

As he entered the room, Brennan noticed the bedside table was filled with handmade Valentine cards. Stop by the flower stand on your way home, he told himself.

He sat by the bed with his briefcase and fished a pencil from his pocket. "How are you today, Miss Adams?"

"Just another sad story, Mr. Brennan." Brennan looked at her, mortified. "Thanks for asking, though."

"I'd like to review your case."

"Of course."

He reached into the briefcase and took out a fat manila envelope. "I've drawn up the complaint and the claim for damages. We'll be asking for a hundred and one thousand dollars. This figure is derived from the extent of your injuries, present and future medical expenses, loss of income, compensation for pain and suffering and, um, loss of personal relationships."

"I don't want their money. What can a hundred thousand dollars buy me?" she cried. "My legs? My career?"

Brennan shook his head. "You can say that only to me, but never to the press or to the public. If the defense hears you say that, they will use it against you."

Brennan said solemnly, "This is a fight for your future. We need to focus on the financial impact of the accident."

He took a deep breath.

"Now, I have identified the following defendants: the corporation that operates the Strand, the New York & San Francisco Amusement Company; the officers, Morris Markowitz, president and general manager, and Moses Lesser, secretary-treasurer; and Basil Knoblock, the stagehand responsible for the fly system at the Strand that night. I've added a phrase allowing us to add others we might discover at a later date."

Silence.

"Do you agree?" Brennan asked.

"Yes."

"The complaint reads: 'Plaintiff alleges that on January 10, 1925, the New York & San Francisco Amusement Company owned and operated the Strand Theater; and that on January 10, 1925, the plaintiff was performing at the Strand Theater as an employee of Will King's entertainment troupe; and that on January 10, 1925, the plaintiff was lawfully standing backstage at the Strand Theater; that she was injured as a result of a failure of equipment owned, operated, and maintained by the New York & San Francisco Amusement Company; that, as a result of the defendants' failure to properly operate and maintain the equipment, plaintiff sustained severe, grievous, and permanent bodily injury; and that the New York & San Francisco Amusement Company, its officers, and employee Basil Knoblock were careless and negligent in operating the Strand Theater, without regard to the safety and rights of the plaintiff.'"

He paused and scrutinized his client. She looked tired. He carefully placed the complaint back in the envelope and handed it to her. "Do you have any questions?"

She took hold of the envelope without looking at it. "No."

"Very good. Go over it today, and I'll arrange to call you tomorrow."

The heavy silence filled the room.

"There's one more item I want to discuss. I hope you won't find this rude."

Her eyes met his gaze. "Go on."

"I want you and John Davis to publicly break off your marriage plans."

That evening, John Davis headed into the hospital with a dozen red roses, looking older than his forty-five years. He hadn't been sleeping much.

He heard calls for nitroglycerin as he walked down the corridor, an emergency in one of the rooms. As Davis pushed open the door to Room 46, a glance at the bed told him Ruby was asleep. She always looked so painfully still.

As he placed the roses in a vase on the side table, he envisioned her running to greet him— smiling, laughing, tugging at his collar pin. She was so effervescent; she always made him think of Champagne.

The cast-iron radiator made its usual hissing noise.

"How's the rest of the world?" Ruby asked sleepily.

"Waiting for your return, my sweet." He kissed

her. She looked so young, with her hair pulled back with a rose-colored bandeau that matched the bed jacket over her body cast. The young nurse had washed her hair. "You take the days as easily as the flowers take the sun. Happy Valentine's Day, dear one."

"I've looked better, but Happy Valentine's Day, my love. Thank you for the roses. I'm sorry I wasn't able to get you anything," she said with a sad smile.

"Nonsense, you are all I want," he said as he sat beside her. "I hope you got my message."

"I did. What's your news?"

When he wasn't at the hospital or the club, Davis had been consulting with doctors throughout the country on Ruby's condition. He read every magazine and newspaper article on spinal conditions he could find, he spent hours in medical libraries, he arranged for massage therapists and sought out Eastern-medicine practitioners. It gave him a sense of being in control. Since Ruby's condition hadn't changed, he had started researching custom wheelchairs and had just ordered a beautiful wicker chair from New York. The company had referred him to a doctor in Manhattan who agreed to review her medical file.

"I've spoken to a spinal specialist in New York who had success with a case like yours. Have you heard of Nellie Revell? She's a newspaper columnist who wrote a book about her paralysis and is now walking again."

Ruby nodded.

"I've arranged passage for him on the Broadway Limited. He'll be here in two weeks."

Ruby smiled at the man who was doing everything possible to help her. He always brought her cheer. He walked over to the radio he'd had delivered. Davis had gone through more red tape than he cared to discuss to get the radio into the hospital.

"Tell me what else is new. I want to live vicariously through you."

"Well, the weather is almost bearable, still rainy and cold, but the forecast is for clearer skies. The politicians are still running around like poultry with their heads cut off and they've started taxing street vendors—the shoe shiners and fruit sellers."

"They're going after the big money."

"That's right." It was good to hear the humor in Ruby's voice. "Say, I'm talking with some movie folks about shooting a picture at the club."

"Really? What is it about?"

"A young Jewish man, the son of a cantor wants to become a jazz singer. He puts on blackface and a wig and sings with a quartet and is an instant success."

"They'll film at Coffee Dan's?"

"That's what I am pitching." Davis removed his coat and draped it neatly over the back of the chair. "Listen, Elmer Ohlsen's orchestra is playing tonight from the Whitcomb Hotel ballroom. I'll leave the club early and we can listen together."

The Whitcomb, with its Tiffany glass, Italian

marble columns, and Austrian crystal chandeliers, was across from the Orpheum Theater, a five-minute walk from City Hall. After the earthquake, it had housed the city government and jail for three years; the words *City Hall* were still etched above the entrance, and the jail cells were still in the basement. On Thursday nights, locals and tourists gathered in the grand ballroom, just off the lobby, and danced to music by orchestras led by Paul Whiteman, Art Hickman, and Clyde Doerr, to name a few. Radio station KFRC broadcast the music via a tower on the Whitcomb's roof, allowing people up and down the coast to hear the music as clearly as if they were in the hotel.

That evening, when the orchestra played "Bill," John caressed Ruby's hand, his fingers tracing the contours of hers, remembering when he had first seen Ruby, four years earlier.

Davis had fallen in love that night at the Techau Tavern, which, despite the name, was a high-class café whose fifty-seat dining room featured nightly jazz. It was known for good music and well-cooked food. With two entrances displaying posters that promoted JAZZ, one on Powell Street and the other on Geary, the Tavern drew a good crowd. Davis' basement restaurant was just a block away.

By then, Ruby's career was in full swing. She'd recently hired a publicist, whose work brought her offers from theatrical producers, movie producers, and fashion companies. Her reputation was growing: People in town were talking about her, and she was getting offers as far away as Chicago and New York.

Her singing coach had pointed out that the new music fit her vocal range well, and so Ruby began studying the new jazz songs. That's what she sang with Paul Whiteman, "the King of Jazz," according to the press. By 1921, Whiteman was in New York, but Ruby was still singing numbers that could be classified as jazz: "After You've Gone," "Hard Hearted Hannah," "My Man." That night, she added a new song, "Bill," by a well-known song-writer named Jerome Kern and lyricist P.G. Wodehouse.

Davis sat at a table to the left of the stage, wearing a sharp navy pinstripe suit, white shirt, and maroon silk tie. He was eating alone, exhausted after a weekend with cronies duck hunting near Banning. When a waiter placed a saddle of lamb and a tumbler of ice in front of him, he reached into his breast pocket, withdrew a silver flask, and poured two fingers of whiskey into the glass. A hush fell over the room as the lights dimmed. Davis pulled the brass ashtray across the inlaid wood table, clipped a Cuban cigar, and leaned back in his chair.

As the Rhythm Boys started to play, Ruby peeked out from behind the curtain. "Good crowd," she said to the stage manager.

"Just heard the competition walked in. Coffee Dan's in the house."

"Is that right? Do you know where he's sitting?"

"Table on the left, the one lighting a cigar. I hear he's quite the lady's man."

She looked at the well-dressed man sitting alone at the table and said, "I've been greeted with a little hammering at his restaurant."

The stage manager smiled. "Those bamboo mallets are quite the gimmick, aren't they? Banging on the table for a waiter or greeting people by breaking plates, especially if they take the slide into the restaurant instead of the stairs."

"I think its fun, and I rather like the advertisements: 'Whoopee with your food.' It's a little naughty, and I have to say, it's memorable!"

Ruby was wearing her hair in a marcel wave. The lights were set to make sure the tiny blue sequins on her gown sparkled at every turn, which was important, since a local dress company was sponsoring the show.

As Ruby stepped onto the stage, she began the intro to the song without any accompaniment.

I used to dream that I would discover
The perfect lover someday.

John Davis's dalliances were well known. His recent separation from his wife, Adele, was the result of one such dalliance. Davis was never serious about his affairs; they weren't betrayals, he'd told his wife, just passing fancies. Adele didn't see it that way.

Davis noticed Ruby's big dark eyes and the dimple in her chin, the way her hair shone like jet, the graceful way she moved. She was beautiful and far too young for him. Without looking, he reached for his glass and took a sip. He sat back and smiled, blatantly appreciating her figure and tiny waist. He couldn't help feeling that someday she would make a very attractive Mrs. John J. Davis.

As she sang, Ruby wandered around the room, but when she reached his table, she stopped and sang to him. The man working the spotlight shook his head, unable to get the clunky light to follow her as they had rehearsed.

Ruby placed her red-nailed hand on Davis's table and, with a coy gesture, sang the refrain.

And I can't explain
It's surely not his brain
That makes me thrill—
I love him because he's wonderful,
Because he's just my Bill.

Later that night, Ruby sat in her dressing room staring at a basket of gardenias, with a card tucked into the arrangement that read:

You would be easy to love.
Coffee Dan.

She loved gardenias.

Pursuing her occasionally at first, Davis soon chased her with a fierceness that she could not ignore.

———

At nine o'clock, when the radio broke for a news report from the *San Francisco Bulletin*, Ruby turned to John and said, "Charles Brennan stopped by today. He wanted to review the legal filing. It's on the table in the big envelope. There's something we should discuss," she added. "He wants us to break up publicly."

This caught Davis by surprise. "That's an odd request to come from an attorney."

"He believes I'll look more of a victim if I'm not betrothed to a wealthy man," she said with a grin. "He says as we pursue our legal case, we mustn't let the press or others tell my story."

Discussing the future was never easy anymore. He felt her slipping away. He'd never stopped wanting to marry her, but since the accident, she'd kept putting him off, saying, "It doesn't seem fair to come to a marriage as less than equals."

"I've loved you for years, and I am a better man for loving you," Davis had told her more than once. "I will not let this accident or anything else break us apart."

He looked in her eyes, now much too large for her face. His own face was full of hurt.

"I will agree, but only for the present and for your future, in which I intend to play a large part."

"Don't be angry. It won't change anything. We just need to keep our engagement a secret, that's all," she whispered.

Naturally, the press was attracted to the story. The source was her brother, and therefore the facts were verified. Two days later, the first article appeared in the *San Francisco Chronicle*.

Marriage Plans Cancelled.
Exclusive to the Chronicle
… At the time of Ruby Adams' accident, Miss Adams was to have been married in two months. "She still loves him," explained her brother, C.F. Adams, "and he wanted to marry her anyway, but she felt it wasn't the square thing to do."

◆

Eleven

Ruby listened to the sound of horses' hooves on the street below her room. She closed her eyes and saw the dairy cart, from a town just south of San Francisco, making its daily delivery of fresh milk to the homes and corner markets around the hospital. Two horses, she thought, chestnut, with pale gold manes and soulful eyes. Sleep still came fleetingly. It wasn't insomnia as much as it was difficult to get comfortable. With so little to see, sounds lit up her imagination.

After weeks in bed, Ruby was able to identify every noise in or outside the hospital. She knew the bells used to call doctors, signal the arrival of an ambulance, and identify meal time. From dawn to dusk, bells punctuated the hours. Using her newly developed talent, Ruby correctly identified garbage, bread, and milk trucks as they rumbled up Hyde and Bush Streets. "Like clockwork," she muttered.

These were the games that helped her pass the endless days.

The seamstress in the next room let out a horrible cough, and Ruby wondered if it was tuberculosis. Her eyes slid toward the window. A full moon cast a blue-gray light in the sky. At five o'clock, the first bell rang. This time, she imagined the sisters walking soundlessly, in their white robes and wimples, to chapel for morning prayers.

A moment later, she heard a much closer sound. The door to the room opened slowly, and light from the corridor streamed in. She took a deep breath. No one ever came in at this hour. Footfalls echoed across the room. "Who's there?" she asked, feeling helpless.

A tall figure approached the bed, whispering, "Miss Adams, it's Walter," the stage-door attendant from the Strand.

"You scared me half to death."

"I'm sorry. I need to talk with you," he whispered urgently.

Walter hadn't always attended to the stage door at the Strand. Ten years earlier, he'd been traveling with a minstrel show, until one night a horse shied at a passing automobile and knocked Walter into a lamppost and broke his leg. Now he walked with a limp. Only his love for the theater was unchanged.

As Ruby reached for the chain on the lamp, a deck of playing cards fell to the floor. "Damn it. Walter, can you help me pick those up?"

Walter hesitated for an instant, fumbling with his flat gray cap. This was the first time he had seen her since the accident. She'd always been so self-assured, so carefree and strong, and now she couldn't even pick up a pack of cards, he thought. There was no mistaking her eyes, but her face was pale and gaunt.

The radiator let go a cough and a whistle, and steam began to seep into the room as Walter replaced the cards on the metal table. "I needed to see you. My wife and I are catching the train to Chicago this morning. Her family's there. She says we gotta get out of town."

"Walter, what's this all about?"

"How much do you know about why the accident happened, Miss Adams?"

"I know that a five-foot woman doesn't stand a chance against a three-hundred-pound sandbag. Why?"

Walter tried to smile. "Well, after your accident, I found the sandbag that fell on you. The rope...it was rotted through. It looked like it had been up in those rafters for a hundred years." He closed his eyes for a moment and pictured Basil Knoblock as he'd often returned from the alley. Then he opened his eyes and said, "I'm not sure Basil has been inspecting the equipment with a clear head."

Ruby's hand tightened into a ball.

Three bells rang out, and they heard footsteps hurrying down the corridor. Another bell rang;

soon nurses would be wheeling the medicine carts for the early-morning rounds. Walter turned when he heard people walking past Ruby's door.

"Later that night, I called to Officer Minna and told him to take a look at the sandbag for his report. But when I went back to where I'd last seen it, it was gone."

"Gone?" Ruby felt her head sway and leaned back against the pillow.

"Sure 'nough—just a trail of sand leading to the alley."

Ruby looked at her trusted friend for an explanation. "Who would have moved it, and why?"

"There was a lot going on that night, but I swear that I noticed a man I've only seen once or twice before backstage."

"Who?"

"That's the thing. That's why my wife says we gotta go to her people. I saw a picture of him in the newspaper lately. You know a man named Pete McDonough?"

"The bail bondsman?"

"Yes."

"Why?"

"Let's just say that since Mr. Finck arrived at the theater, there've been all sorts of shady characters around. He keeps some very bad company. I figure maybe Basil knows something about this and that's why he's been able to keep his job. You know he drinks?"

Ruby nodded. "Yes, but—"

"I've seen a lot in forty years, Miss Adams, and I think Mr. Lesser and Mr. Markowitz only care about the box-office receipts and don't know what's really happening backstage, if you know what I mean. A bunch of no-goodniks is what they are."

"Walter, who've you told about this?"

"Just the missus."

"You need to tell the authorities."

"I told Officer Minna that the sandbag was gone, but he just looked at me cross-eyed. Authorities don't listen to a man like me, Miss Adams."

Ruby looked up at the ceiling fan. She had to tell Charles; she had to tell John.

A bell in the corridor seemed to startle Walter. "I'm sorry, Miss Adams. I didn't mean to scare you, but I thought you should know. I have to leave now. God bless you." He took her hand, then turned away. At the door, his figure was backlit, illuminated by the lights in the corridor. He put on his cap and lifted a hand in goodbye, and then slipped out, leaving Ruby alone and vulnerable in her hospital bed.

Across San Francisco Bay, in Oakland, the 16th Street Station was the link between the Bay Area and the rest of the country. At the Ferry Building, Walter paused and peered up at the seven o'clock ferry. His wife was already onboard. When the boat's horn blew, he urged his legs up the ramp. The morning was bitterly cold, and his leg was stiff. He tugged the cap down over his ears. In forty minutes, he and his wife would be on a train and would not be returning. "God bless!" he whispered.

At the hospital, Ruby's eyes filled with tears. She recalled standing in front of the stage door that night, watching Basil Knoblock drinking from a flask. Was she the victim of a careless stagehand? Then she remembered what Walter had said about the sandbag and Pete McDonough, the kingpin of the Tenderloin. According to John, the man had his fingers in many pies. Could he really have some sort of tie to the theater?

—⁓—

Carrie had been trying to track down the police report for weeks. Brennan had left messages for Captain Hoertkorn, commander of the Southern Police Station, but hadn't heard anything. Now, with the news that Pete McDonough had been backstage that night, and about Walter's fear of the theater owners, Brennan scrambled to the station. It was South of the Slot, slang for Market Street, at Third and Bryant. He got there around eight-thirty and noticed Old Glory was flapping in the wind at half-mast.

The city was mourning the death of Michael de Young, who with his brother had founded what became the *San Francisco Chronicle*. His death was the talk of the town. All the major newspapers had put the story on the front page, and the *Chronicle* printed a special section. Even the city courts were closed, out of respect.

Brennan marveled at how a man can be in good health one day and dead the next. That made him think of Ruby. One minute, she was singing and dancing, a grand career ahead of her; the next minute, she was crippled for life.

He shook his head and entered the station. The mostly bare walls were a cheerless, dirty beige. Behind the metal bars separating the public from the criminals was an equally cheerless sergeant in a thread-bare dark blue uniform. His hair was a grayish white that made him look as if he'd been on the job for years. Brennan told him he was there to see Captain Hoertkorn and took a seat on an ancient metal chair.

The telephone bell rang constantly, and drunks were yelling somewhere in the back. The chair was so uncomfortable, he walked across the cement floor and peered out the window. A paddy wagon was idling at the corner. A beat cop stepped off the running board, and the wagon drove off.

Before filing the complaint with the court, Brennan wanted to ask the police, again, whether a report had been filed the night of the accident. The stage-door attendant had told Ruby the beat cop had come in the theater, but Carrie had been informed that no police report existed. Were the police stonewalling? If the officer had made a note of the condition of the sandbag and rope, it would solidify the claim of negligence.

Brennan found himself humming *Rhapsody in Blue*. He couldn't get the melody out of his head. Ruby said that humming Gershwin was a new type of flu, "a national epidemic," she'd called it.

He was distracted by a thick-waisted, red-haired prostitute shouting in Russian at a middle-aged man as a couple of police officers ushered the two through the door to the cells. The sergeant hollered, "Captain will be out to see you in a few minutes."

With a full head of salt-and-pepper hair and a strong-looking build, Hoertkorn appeared a distinguished officer of the law. "Let me guess. You're looking for coffee and a doughnut," he bellowed at Brennan, lifting black eyebrows the size of caterpillars.

Brennan stood up and laughed. "You know me too well, Tom."

"Come on, we'll see if we have a clean mug. Sorry about all this," he added, indicating the prostitutes and drunks in the long corridor. "Last night we had three burglaries and a homicide, and we're always cleaning up the petty crime. Did you see that de Young died after surgery on his appendix?" Hoertkorn asked as they walked to his office.

"The moral of that story is, you can have all the money in the world, eat the best food, hire the finest doctors, but when your number's up, it is up."

"Very true," said Hoertkorn. "The man cheated death, when Spreckels took objection to something he wrote in the *Chronicle* and a shot at him."

As Brennan sat down in Hoertkorn's office, the wall shook and a man cried out in pain. "You guys violating someone's rights out there?" Brennan asked.

"I didn't hear a thing," said Hoertkorn. He made a loud slurping sound as he took a sip of weak coffee. "All right, what's up?"

"Tom, I'm looking for the police report made at the Strand Theater on the night of January 10."

Hoertkorn gave him a dubious look. "This about Ruby Adams, Charlie?"

"Yes."

Hoertkorn ran a hand through his bushy hair. "The folks at the theater called an ambulance, not us. Believe me, with a popular showgirl like that, I'd remember."

"That doesn't quite jive with what others are saying. I have it from a witness that Officer Minna stopped by."

"Hold your horses. Who told you that?"

Hoertkorn regarded Brennan and then picked up a message on his desk.

"Do you know the de Youngs called requesting a police escort for the funeral procession from St. Mary's to Colma? Can you believe it? We have crime to fight! I told them to call Chief Murray over at the Fire Department."

"Tom, come on. Can you check?"

"Okay. Give me a minute," Hoertkorn replied. "I'll be right back."

"Take your time," said Brennan, leaning back in his chair.

Of all the police captains in the San Francisco precincts, Hoertkorn had always been a valuable cog in the city machine, at the center of the city's graft. An eclectic array of tea salons, restaurants, brothels, and cafes paid the police for the benefit of selling and serving liquor. Many knew him to be personally connected to two bookie joints and a couple of speakeasies in the Mission District. His friends and fellow officers saw him as a charming, friendly, no-bull policeman, but he had a mean streak.

Hoertkorn returned to the office and announced, "Well, that was a paper chase, Charlie. If Minna was there, he didn't write a report."

Brennan looked unconvinced.

"Charlie, I think it's time for you to drop this line of inquiry. The police are the good guys, remember? Ruby Adams found herself in the wrong place at the wrong time."

"The way you put it makes it sound like it was her fault."

"Nonsense! That's up to the court to decide."

Rather than belabor the point, Brennan prepared to leave for his office, where he would focus on writing a comprehensive complaint. "Well, Tom, thanks for the coffee."

That afternoon, Brennan took one last look at the complaint for the Summons of Ruby Adams vs. New York & San Francisco Amusement Company and handed the thick ochre-colored envelope to Carrie, who would arrange for a courier to pick it up and file the documents.

Superior Court was on the fourth floor of the beautiful Beaux Arts-style City Hall, which just ten years earlier had replaced the government building destroyed in the earthquake. The vast space covered two city blocks; the dome, rising three hundred and seven feet above the street, was said to be higher than that of the United States Capitol building. Its famed architect, Arthur Brown, Jr., had paid great attention to the finishing details, such as gilded doors, gold lamps, even the fonts used in signage.

The courier turned the brass doorknob and stepped into the court clerk's office. The clerk reviewed the paperwork from under his green eyeshade, accepted the two-dollar fee, and stamped and signed the documents. As soon as the courier left, the clerk placed the CLOSED sign behind the door's frosted-glass window and slipped into an empty office. He listened to the door snap shut and drew the shade, then reached for the telephone.

"Operator, can I help you?"

"Please connect me to the editorial department of the *San Francisco Examiner*..... Yes, I'll wait."

Soon he was speaking intently into the mouthpiece. "It's Harold. I just accepted the forms for a lawsuit against the Strand Theater.... What? Yes, Ruby Adams....A hundred and one thousand bucks. How soon will I get the money?"

He hung up the telephone and grinned.

◆

Twelve

Markowitz and his wife left the Hotel Ritz in time to board the morning train at Gare Saint-Lazare for Cherbourg, where they boarded the RMS *Olympic* for New York. On that journey, Morris reflected how happy his wife was shopping and experiencing Paris. He found an inner satisfaction that he was able to give her things that made her happy. But when, the lead passenger ship for the White Star Line hit choppy water off the coast of Scotland. Juliette became ill and begged off dinner, so he and Carl Laemmle dined alone.

For all intents and purposes, the Markowitz's were assimilated into society. Jews ran the entertainment industry; however, Morris insisted on adhering to a kosher lifestyle. This angered his wife. She believed it opened the family up to anti-Semitism. But, Morris was disciplined as an Eastern Orthodox and found one cook of the sixty onboard, who prepared and served kosher.

"What luck to see you on the manifest," Markowitz had cabled Laemmle, as if he had happened to peruse the list and was surprised to find Laemmle on it. Like Markowitz, Laemmle wore a black tuxedo and batwing collar. He was a short, stout man with a round face. The logo for his first production company had been a gremlin; many joked that the artist had based the drawing on him. He was a family man who still spoke lovingly of his departed wife, whose departure, however, had given him more time to play cards, his one vice. Sid Grauman was one of Laemmle's weekly bridge and poker partners.

At dinner, Laemmle tried to describe one of his studio's recently completed pictures. "Did you ever try to tell someone how good something was and find yourself simply lost at sea, without half enough of the right kind of words to express your enthusiasm? That's how I feel about *Phantom of the Opera*."

Morris rubbed his chin and treated himself to a chocolate nonpareil. He was surprised at Laemmle's enthusiasm. Universal was known as a bread-and-butter company, rarely aimed at admired works. Maybe he was just trying to match the success of *The Hunchback of Notre Dame*, also starring Lon Chaney, which Laemmle had produced two years earlier. Then again, the studio had called the movie its "super jewel."

"All right, son. Lay your cards on the table, face up."

Morris hadn't been expecting such an abrupt change of subject. "Well, uh…you know the Strand is one of the best theaters in San Francisco."

Laemmle nodded. "She's a beauty."

"It's perfectly positioned for the right company. I…."

Laemmle leaned forward. "Morris, what's up your sleeve? You want Universal to buy the Strand?"

Markowitz smiled sadly. "I can't fight the likes of moguls like Fox, Zukor, and Mayer, the way they control the distribution and advertising of their pictures. They force these bookings on us; you have to take the turkeys with the jewels. Problem is, no one wants to see the turkeys, so we have to lower the ticket prices. Well, my partner and I, we're tired, and we're looking to sell." He pulled out his gold cigarette case and looked at Laemmle. "Universal would be able to show its motion pictures in a topnotch theater in the center of San Francisco."

"Son, that's a most appealing offer. I'm especially attracted to the location. You can't buy property on Market Street anymore. It's a valuable theater, that's for sure. If you're serious…."

"I'm serious."

"Well, I'm sure you know all the first-run theaters are being purchased by the likes of Zukor, Fox, and Loew." Laemmle took a sip of his brandy and cleared his throat. "I don't like to tie up that much capital, but…. Hmmm. What's your price?"

Markowitz had his price ready. His blue eyes flickered. He took his time placing his cigarette in an ashtray and then finding a business card as Laemmle waited.

"Do you need a pen?" Laemmle asked.

"Thanks, I have one," Markowitz said, which he used to scribble a dollar sign and six numbers on the back of the card.

The number lit up Laemmle's eyes. Morris could see Laemmle considering the number, staring at the card a little longer than he needed to. "It's a lot of money. If we're going to do this, I'll have to consider paying part of it in stock."

"I'm sure my partner and I will find any offer worth considering."

"All right. I'll have my attorney draw up terms as soon as we're back in New York, and we can go from there."

"I'm looking forward to doing business with you...again."

—⁓—

Several days later, as the cold salt air slapped his face, Morris buttoned his fur-trimmed Ulster coat and smiled at the sweeping New York City skyline, just beyond the Port of New York. He smoothed his ever-increasing gray hair as the ship's engines ground down, a horn from a tugboat blasted, a fireboat spouted water. The *Olympic* was docked at Pier 59, beside the massive White Star Line terminal. The wood-and-glass structure had a lookout deck on which friends and families swarmed to catch a glimpse of their loved ones as they descended the ship's gangway.

He and Juliette were anxious to see their golden-haired four-year-old daughter. Morris had promised to take her to the giant carousel in Golden Gate Park and buy her some caramel corn as soon as he returned.

"Has Uncle Carl gone ashore?" Juliette asked, joining Morris in a smart new cashmere overcoat.

"No, he said he had business to take care of before leaving the ship."

"Do you know why I like him?"

"Hmm? No, why?"

"Because he's a German Jew and treats us Eastern European Jews like family."

"Yes, he does," Morris agreed, throwing his cigarette into the Hudson River. "Shall we?"

As Morris oversaw their steamer trunks and small luggage being loaded onto a handcart, he was surprised to hear his name. "Telegram for Mr. Morris Markowitz!" a young man in a khaki uniform and brown leather boots was shouting above the din.

"Yes! Here I am!"

"Telegram."

Markowitz dipped into his pocket for a tip. "I'm sorry, I only have a few French coins."

"Aww, that's okay. I have a bunch of those coins at home. My mom says they aren't worth much."

February 28, 1925
Mr. Morris Markowitz
URGING YOU TO RETURN TO SAN

FRANCISCO IMMEDIATELY (STOP) LAWSUIT
AGAINST NY&SF CO. FILED BY RUBY ADAMS
(STOP)
  M. LESSER

"What is it, darling?" Juliette asked.

His face ashen, Morris handed the telegram to his wife. Morris had been so worried and distracted lately; it was more and more difficult to reach him. As she read the cable, Juliette realized the pressure of the accident had been building. Worse, it would continue to do so.

That afternoon, the Markowitzes boarded the Pennsylvania Railroad's Broadway Limited. The route would take them to Philadelphia and on to Washington, arriving in Chicago the following morning. After stashing their bags in their sleeping compartment, they found a table in the dining car. Morris had said little. Now he took out a notepad and composed a cable.

  Moses Lesser
  RETURNING IMMEDIATELY (STOP) DUE IN SF
IN 5 DAYS (STOP)

The train was packed with revelers who would be attending the presidential inauguration, in Washington, D.C.

"I really wish we'd thought about attending the inauguration, don't you?" Juliette said as she watched two women walk by waving "Keep Coolidge" flags.

"Indeed, those people are definitely on the Coolidge Prosperity bandwagon. But I'm afraid these recent events require me to get home as soon as possible." He waved to the conductor, negotiating his way through the dining car to announce the next stop. "Excuse me," Markowitz called. "Can you wire this for me?"

The conductor put his timepiece away and said, "Yes, sir."

"And do you have today's newspaper?"

"Yes, sir."

Turning back to Juliette, Morris said, "After being abroad, I'd like to see what's going on in this country, wouldn't you?"

The train whistle sounded and the car lurched forward on the iron tracks. A few minutes later, Morris was scanning the *New York World-Telegram.* Headline after headline proclaimed the prosperity of the nation. "Juliette, it says here that in 1923, General Motors sold over eight hundred thousand automobiles." He whistled softly. "I should invest in General Motors, my dear."

Turning to the last page of the main section, he saw news articles about "Scientists Lost in Brazil," "Governors to View Coolidge's Inaugural," and "$500,000 in Art Stolen from Hollywood Home." He was thinking about owning half a million dollars worth of art when another headline caught his eye.

Injured Actress Asks
$101,429 As Damages

(Associated Press)
SAN FRANCISCO, February 28, 1925—
Charging that her career as a stage dancer was
prematurely ended when a sandbag fell on her
in the wings of the Strand Theater, Miss Ruby
Adams has filed suit against the theater
company and others asking damages of
$101,429. The theater company is designated
as the New York & San Francisco Amusement
Company.

The news had been picked up by the Associated
Press network. It wasn't on the front page, but
still—it was in the main section of the newspaper.
Carl Laemmle and others would soon read the
article, if not in the World-Telegram then in other
papers that paid for AP's national distribution. He
was flabbergasted. Why would the Associated Press
pick this story up?

Looking out the window, he saw the poverty of
life along a railway line. The lean-to shacks with
laundry hanging heavily from backyard clotheslines
reminded him of Romania. Jews had been treated
so terribly there, the pogroms and expulsions as
well as everyday anti-Semitism, that his family had
left for a better life in 1885, facing hunger and
more anti-Semitism as they traveled to New York
by way of Greece.

He felt an odd sensation in his chest and began to
perspire. "What is it, Morris?" Juliette asked, her
hand on his shoulder.

He handed her the newspaper and said, "The ax has fallen."

—◠◠◠—

Normally, Morris Markowitz was in his office above the Strand by ten a.m. Now it was closer to eleven, and he had been in bed for three days. He'd picked up an awful flu on the train from Chicago. Now he sat at his desk, feeling little energy to deal with the problems that faced him.

The organist was practicing, as usual, as he surveyed the papers that had piled up. Morris lit a cigarette as he looked at the ledger and the last month of box-office receipts. The average ticket price was twenty-five cents, and it looked as if the theater was making money off Fox's Tom Mix westerns. Though the Strand didn't show his most recent films, the cowboy star, with his tall white hat and clean-cut features, was at the peak of his popularity. According to *Film Daily*, only Harold Lloyd and Gloria Swanson were more popular stars. People got a kick watching Mix and his horse, Tony, jump twenty feet over canyon cuts.

The intercom buzzed. "Colonel Herbert Choynski and Mr. Lesser are here to meet with you, Mr. Markowitz," his secretary said.

Choynski was a formidable, if not notorious, attorney whose title dated to the Spanish-American War, the son of a pioneering newspaper publisher from Germany who had criticized the city's Bavarian Jewish establishment. His legal career had spanned four decades of rude, combative behavior that left him with hypertension and an arthritic body that cracked and ached when he walked.

Choynski walked slowly into the office and held out his hand. "Colonel Herbert Choynski, young man. Howd'ja do? As I was just telling Moses, this is a very unfortunate occurrence we have here."

"Yes," Morris agreed, shaking Choynski's arthritic hand.

"To think that a chorus girl would sue for an injury that was probably her own fault. Yes, plaintiffs are frequently at fault in these types of cases," Choynski said, his mouth half-hidden by a sizeable Prussian mustache that might have been dashing before his dark hair turned a yellowish gray.

"Oh? Interesting." The man is ruthless, Morris thought.

"Yes, indeed. Plaintiffs usually contribute to these types of incidents. At times, a third party is at fault."

"Perhaps we should all sit down and discuss this," Morris said, politely directing the men to take a seat. Choynski spent a moment inspecting all the posters. Then he reached into his briefcase and removed some papers. He had had a law clerk pull some information about the accident, mostly news articles, he told Markowitz and Lesser. In his opinion, the accident was a result of the girl standing where she didn't belong.

Turning to Moe Lesser, he said, "Your father,

with his Russian blood, is surely an ancestor on my mother's side and is a very good friend of mine, Moses. My office will prepare a defense as solidly for you as we would for my own son. We will deny all the allegations."

Choynski turned to Markowitz. "Son, I never lose my client's money. Your assets are as important to me as if they were my own."

The partners looked at each other and smiled.

"We will begin by denying everything and claiming that the plaintiff was at fault. We will question the girl's character. It's all about character, you see. Why, I know actors better than I know myself! An actor's ambition in life is to see his face on the front page of the daily news. Publicity to such women is bliss, and lack of it is despair. The spotlight is her dream," he went on, as if already orating in court, "and the horizon of her hope bounded by the row of heads at her feet."

Markowitz cleared his throat uneasily. "Colonel, the people of San Francisco love Ruby Adams, which means they'll want to take care of her. I'm not sure we can paint her as an actress just looking for attention."

Choynski's eyes turned cold. "My good man, I'm not hoping to convince the public overnight, that would be a tall order. But over time, we'll change the public's perception. A little adverse publicity should help. Granted, there's a lot of sympathy for the girl right now, and we need to change that! You see, the public is very fickle, my boy."

When Markowitz started to speak, Lesser glared at him.

"Why, she's nothing more than a glorified chorus girl," Choynski proclaimed. "Let's see if she's been in trouble with the authorities. Have there been any improprieties? Does she have any secrets? The public has a thirst for gossip, and scandal sheets are a dime a dozen. Moses, can you talk to your cronies? Maybe that Poultney fellow who works for McDonough." George Poultney wrote slanderous articles under the pseudonym Dick the Rounder.

"I don't know Poultney," Lesser said.

"Don't be ridiculous, son! Your father confided in me that you played handball with him just the other day." Choynski paused. "I can speak with him if you don't want to." Somehow, Markowitz knew that wasn't an option.

Lesser looked down. "I'll put a call in to him."

Moe Lesser was never terribly discerning about the company he kept, Markowitz thought. Figures he knows Dick the Rounder.

"We need to look for anything that might indicate Ruby Adams is not quite the darling of the stage we think she is."

Lesser saw where the Colonel was going with this line of thinking. "I hear the girl's been in a honey relationship with Coffee Dan."

The Colonel looked puzzled.

"They're cohabitating," Moe clarified.

"Ah, good—a floozy, a tart, that's what we need. Let's get some articles that'll paint this girl in a less than flattering light. Put the plaintiff on the defense is what I say!" he exclaimed.

Choynski leaned back in his chair and turned serious.

"Asking for a hundred thousand dollars is preposterous. Why, it's grossly excessive. To win this case, they must prove three things," he began, pushing back his index finger. "First, that the theater owners had a duty to keep the actress safe and without harm while on your premises. Next, that you breached that legal duty. And finally, that the plaintiff was injured as a result of your actions or inactions.

"Obviously, she was injured, but was it your responsibility to provide a safe place for her to work? I believe there are precedents that say no. I'll prove, beyond a doubt, that her own actions contributed to her injury. As I say, we'll deny all allegations and make them prove everything."

Choynski studied a list he'd brought. "I'll need to take a look at the contracts with Will King's troupe."

Morris saw the fierceness in his eyes. He had read a little about Choynski. He had come to prominence raising funds for the San Francisco Relief effort after the earthquake and had a younger brother, Joe, who was once "the foremost Jewish boxer of San Francisco." Clearly, he was a fighter, too. But he had as many enemies as friends.

Markowitz pressed the button on the intercom. "Daisy, please bring in the Will King contracts. And tell the organist to take a break from practicing for an hour."

"Yes, Mr. Markowitz."

Choynski took out a handkerchief and blew his nose, then continued, "Now, the plaintiff's attorney is Charles Brennan. I've seen him around the courthouse. He's a good trial lawyer, loves the limelight, but I have it on good authority that his paperwork can be less than stellar. We'll delay the proceedings. Drown them in paper. That'll give us time to publish a few juicy tidbits." Choynski looked as if he were enjoying himself. "You boys have heard the adage 'Justice delayed is justice denied'?"

"You don't mean you want to prolong this?" Morris asked. He was already worried the adverse press would affect ticket sales.

"Yes, we'll buttonhole the conversation; you know, tell the other side of the story."

"I hear John Davis—Coffee Dan—is paying her medical bills," Lesser said.

"Is that a fact? Coffee Dan's, that's that ham-and-egger on O'Farrell, correct?"

"Yes."

"Something tells me a few raids may cause undue financial stress on his establishment." Choynski took a pad of paper from his briefcase and ruminated for a moment. "Now, can you tell me what kind of insurance you have?"

Markowitz looked at his partner. "I'm afraid you've hit upon a tricky bit."

"What is the tricky bit?"

"As of the moment, we carry a liability policy of five thousand dollars," Markowitz said, still looking at Lesser. Moe had recommended reducing the insurance premium just last year.

"Five grand? That would barely cover a slip-and-fall on the sidewalk!"

"Well, it's been a difficult year. The premiums are expensive, and we wanted to keep costs down... and profits up," Moe added with a cunning grin.

"I see. Listen, boys, I'm here to protect you from the courts. That's what Herbert Choynski does! Why, if this goes to trial and she gets a sympathetic judge.... Well, let's just say the gas-pipe robbers will have your money in no time. You need to know that they can put a lien on your property and make untangling assets impossible. Is that what you want?" he said loudly.

The men shook their heads.

"I say the best thing to do is prolong the proceedings and give you boys time to safeguard your assets."

While the conversation made him feel a little ill, Morris thought the Colonel was very shrewd. He picked up the summons from his desk and read it.

**Superior Court of California,
San Francisco County**

Plaintiff: Ruby Adams
Nature of Action: Damages
Defendant: New York & San Francisco
Amusement Corp., et al.
   Plaintiffs Attorney: Charles H. Brennan, 785
Market Street, 9th floor, San Francisco,
California

You are hereby summoned to answer the
complaint in this action, and to serve a copy of
your answer, or demurrer, within thirty days
after the service of this summons. Failure to
answer will result in judgment taken against
you by default for the relief demanded in the
complaint.
                                    February 19, 1925
                                    Charles H. Brennan
                                    Attorney for Plaintiff

"Demurrer?" Morris asked, contemplating the
complaint.

"It means to object to the claim on grounds other
than denying the facts stated in the complaint,"
Choynski explained. "So here's what we will do.
We'll file for an extension just short of the thirty
days required. Then we'll file for an extension after
that. Finally, we'll file demurrers for each defendant
named in the complaint. That should take us
through May."

His clients were silent.

"Is there a police report?" Choynski asked.

"The police report seems to be missing," Lesser

told him with that grin.

Markowitz's eyes swept from Choynski to Lesser. "The police report is missing?"

"That's what I hear," Lesser said smugly.

"Good!" Choynski said as he scratched an item off his list with a flourish. "Now, hand me the contracts. I'll need to go over them with a fine-tooth comb." The Colonel looked back at his list.

"Tell me, who is this Basil Knoblock?"

"He's one of our stagehands," Morris told him.

Choynski looked at Markowitz and asked, "Is the company prepared to represent him, I mean cover his legal costs?"

"That's something we'll need to discuss," Lesser said quickly. "The boy is young and a bit of a dullard. I suppose he will need some counsel."

"How will it end for Basil?" Choynski muttered.

"Pardon?" Markowitz asked.

"Well, as I said, many times in these civil cases, a third party may be at fault. Say the company that makes the equipment."

"Well, Basil is responsible for maintaining the equipment."

"Hmm. All right. Let me think on that."

Choynski stood, using the arms of his chair as leverage. "Moses, I believe you're joining us for Sabbath dinner. Edith's cooking her braised brisket with onions and mushrooms!"

"Yes, I know my father is looking forward to it."

◆

Thirteen

The officers of the New York & San Francisco Amusement Company agreed that the best course of action was for Choynski to slow everything down. After the court denied the defendants their requested demurrer, it gave them ten days to answer the complaint. The defendants asked for thirty days to craft a reply, and the court granted their request.

Meanwhile, Lesser worked with McDonough and Poultney to plant "items" about Ruby and Coffee Dan. As expected, Carl Laemmle's attorney had called, once the lawsuit made news, to say he was no longer interested in buying the Strand. Markowitz was spending most of his time seeking another buyer. Juliette hardly saw him. He locked himself in his office for hours, making telephone calls to a list of potential buyers: William Fox, Marcus Loew, Jack Warner at Warner Bros., Adolph Zukor at Paramount.

Zukor made Markowitz think of Herb Rothchild, who worked with the Paramount-Publix theater chain. He had to be doing well. Early on, Rothchild, an attorney, had developed the California Theatre, near the eastern end of Market Street; it was on a tiny lot but, with its Gothic design and impressive Wurlitzer organ, it was considered the city's first real movie palace. Four years later, under the Publix banner, he'd opened the Granada, across the street from the Strand. And just last year, he'd unveiled a Classical Revival building with a sixty-eight-foot tower south of the Slot, where workmen for Rothchild Entertainment created stage and film sets.

Both Rothchild and Markowitz were members of Temple Emanu-El, which claimed to be the oldest Jewish congregation west of the Mississippi. The members had asked one of the city's most renowned architects, Arthur Brown, Jr.—who had designed both City Hall and the War Memorial Opera House, just across the street—to design a bigger temple for them on the western side of the city. Markowitz had seen the blueprints, in what Brown called the Byzantine Revival style; the building's huge dome, he'd heard, was inspired by the Hagia Sofia, in Istanbul. Imagine that, he always thought, a Jewish temple influenced by a Greek Orthodox Church that became a Muslim mosque.

One evening, he and Juliette went to a fundraiser in the current temple, on Union Square. He was hoping Rothchild would be there. In the reception hall, he was watching some young boys jockeying at the buffet table when he saw him from the corner of his eye. Herbert Rothchild was tall and lean and handsome, with olive skin, high cheekbones, and a Roman nose. He was loading his plate with slices of tongue and pastrami, chopped chicken liver and bagels, when the boys jostled him and he dropped an egg bagel. The boys laughed and ran out to the courtyard.

Morris picked up the bagel and placed it on a corner of the table. "Are you feeding an army, Herb?" he joked.

"Ha. Morris, you are on to me," Rothchild said with a Bavarian accent.

"Do you have a minute, Herb?" Markowitz indicated a corner of the room, safe from eavesdroppers and celebrants. "Let's talk over there."

Rothchild nodded convivially and followed Markowitz to an overstuffed sofa.

"How are things going with the brass at Paramount?" Markowitz asked.

"I'm at the highest levels there."

Markowitz smiled. "Which is one reason I wanted to talk to you. I'm looking for a buyer for the Strand."

"You boys want to sell?"

"Yes. Yes, we do."

A few weeks later, under a dome of blue skies, some board members of Temple Emanu-El were at the construction site, at the corner of Lake and

Arguello Streets. Touring the site offered an opportunity for the lay leaders of the Reform congregation to meet with the city's civic and business leaders to shape the future of the temple.

Markowitz took a *kippah* from the basket and covered his head, stood against the back wall and looked at the group of elders praying in the sanctuary. In front of him, Rothchild was standing next to Herbert Fleishhacker, a generous donor. Their faces were radiant with self-congratulations having successfully accomplished the task of building a new temple. Markowitz's blue eyes flickered as he walked up the aisle and sidled next to Rothchild.

"Looks like they're making good progress. Should be open soon."

"Yes, indeed," Rothchild said pleasantly.

"Herb, do you mind if we talk business here at the temple?"

"Of course not. The Gentiles have the Masons; the Jews have their temple. But it's such a nice day. Let's take a walk."

They crossed the loggia and walked through an iron gate to the open courtyard recently planted with olive trees and rosemary, reaching the street just as a noisy streetcar turned the corner.

"Here is what I know," Rothchild said. "Publix wants to be the largest theater operator in the world. The company's looking for additional theaters in the downtown area of San Francisco, and with its seventeen hundred seats, the Strand looks attractive to them."

Rothchild pointed and turned down Lake Street as he continued talking.

"I received a confidential memorandum this morning. It outlines an offer to purchase all assets of your company. Everything—lock, stock, and barrel—if they can finance the purchase with a combination of cash and stock. And there's an additional requirement."

Markowitz took a deep breath. "What?"

"This matter must be handled quietly. There's to be absolutely no publicity," Rothchild said in a lower voice. "You must not divulge the name of the buyer to anyone but your business partners."

They walked in silence for a moment along the quiet residential street. Markowitz opened his gold cigarette case and offered a cigarette to Rothchild. Rothchild shook his head.

"I understand."

"Herman Wobber is the West Coast representative coordinating this deal for Publix, but all decisions are being made in New York. Everyone reports to Sam Dembow. If you and your partner agree that the terms are acceptable, I'll make the call on Monday."

So it appeared Adolph Zukor would not be directly involved in the transaction. This was disappointing. Markowitz had hoped to meet the man and possibly parlay the introduction into an opportunity.

"Herman's a solid fellow," Morris said.

"There's one other detail."

"Go on."

"We're going to need help from someone in the city tax office. We want to make sure the change of property ownership is also done quietly."

Morris couldn't help but smile. "I'm sure Colonel Choynski can handle that. I'll speak with Moe and let you know tomorrow if he's on board."

Back at the construction site, Markowitz dropped his cigarette on a granite step and crushed it with a newly purchased Italian leather shoe.

"Well," he said thoughtfully, "it sounds like the Strand will be in good hands. That's important to me, Herb."

They shook hands, and Morris turned and walked past piles of dirt and sand. Then he gave an enormous sigh and jogged across the street to his automobile. He felt a mixture of elation and sadness. The Strand had been his baby for eight years, and he would miss her. He looked at his watch; it was approaching three o'clock, giving him just enough time to call Moe before he went to *mikvah*, the ritual bath on Sacramento Street.

———

A few days later, Lesser and Markowitz reviewed the agreement. The deal would be done by a company to be incorporated in a matter of days, which would purchase the Strand for seven hundred thousand dollars in a fifty-fifty split of cash and stock. This included transfer of all assets, theatrical equipment, chairs, projectors, organ, and everything else. Rothchild would receive a commission of ten percent. The figure wasn't as high as they had wanted, but they were selling damaged goods. Once the deal was signed and money delivered, the New York & San Francisco Amusement Company would have no tangible assets.

"This says Publix. Why aren't they doing this deal under Paramount-Publix?" Lesser asked.

"There's nothing unusual about it. They want to keep it separate from their theater across the street, and away from the watchful eye of the government and the Federal Trade Commission. And you and I must keep the purchaser quiet. We cannot divulge the names I mentioned earlier."

"Won't people be suspicious? They'll be showing Paramount's pictures."

"From what I understand, they'll give preference to Paramount pictures, but negotiate with all the production studios. Do we have an agreement?" Markowitz asked his partner, knowing the faint feeling of loss must be apparent on his face.

"Yes, we do. Congratulations."

On Friday, June 19, 1925, the Strand Realty Company was incorporated. The company, organized under the laws of California for the purpose of real estate, was owned by Paramount-Publix. Sam Dembow, Jr., was named president; someone named P.R. Kent was vice-president.

The following Friday, June 26, 1925, a clerk in San Francisco City Hall quietly recorded the Strand Realty Company's purchase of a property at 965 Market Street.

—⁓—

Within the walls of the Saint Francis Hospital, one patient kept the nurses and nuns on their toes. Musicians, comedians, showgirls, journalists and physicians were beating a path to and from Room 46. The steady flow of visitors required the nuns to be extra vigilant, in order to make sure that Miss Adams was able to get enough rest.

Concerts erupted at various times of the day. Ruby's friends brought instruments and song into the hospital. She shared this good fortune with the nurses, nuns, doctors and patients who assembled outside Room 46. The hospital administrators frowned at first, but their faces quickly softened into a wide smile, as they agreed that the concert was good medicine.

After one of those concerts, about three o'clock in the afternoon, there was a knock on her door. Charles Brennan stepped into the room slowly. With distaste in his mouth, he revealed that the plaintiff was further delaying the court process.

Twenty minutes into the discussion the nurses noticed Ruby's voice.

"I can't believe the defendants have postponed these proceedings again! My savings are being swallowed up quickly." Ruby told her lawyer impatiently.

"Yes, I'm afraid so," Brennan said, standing by her bed gazing at an open box of candy on the bedside table. "What are these?"

"Caramels."

"They have to answer the complaint," he reminded her, lifting a caramel from the box. "After that, I will ask the defendants to disclose their assets."

"Well, I wouldn't hold my breath, if I were you," Ruby said. "This is like death by a thousand delays. Charles," she went on, "I'd like to take a more active role in my case. I've never been one to sit back and watch. Do you have any books I can read? It might help me understand how the courts and the jury system work."

Charles knew Ruby was a quick study, and this might take her mind off the troubles Choynski and his cheapskate clients were compounding. "Yes," he said, turning to drop into the nearest chair, "I can get—what the devil?!"

One of the musicians, a big practical joker, had left a Whoopi cushion on the seat under a crocheted blanket, and it went off with a loud flatulent sound. Brennan bounced up far more quickly than he'd sat down. He shot an embarrassed glance at Ruby, and the two dissolved into laughter.

It was a full minute before either could speak again. "Oh, that was marvelous," Ruby said, wiping her eyes. "I thought my laughing days were over."

"I should have expected that sooner or later from you."

"What do they say…?" Ruby murmured. "'He who declared it, blared it. He who observed it, served it.' Ha! That's just what I needed, a little bawdy humor to lighten my mood!" She took a deep breath and blew her nose. "I'm sorry, what were you saying?"

———

Late each afternoon, a newsboy made the rounds behind the nurses, selling newspapers to the patients.

"Thousand die in a tornado that hit Missouri and Illinois!" he yelled as he thrust his head into Ruby's room.

The sight of the young newsboy, in his knickers and ragged flat cap, never failed to remind her of the theater and the boys, none more than ten years old, who worked diligently calling out time and running errands.

"I'd say you're a bit of a tornado, Owen."

"That's what my mom said. Want a paper this evening, Miss Adams?"

"Yes, hand me my change purse, over on the dresser, will you?"

The boy reached across the boxes of chocolates and picked up the petit-point purse. "Are you going to eat all those chocolates, Miss Adams?"

"Certainly not. I don't want to get fat on top of everything else! Help yourself to some candy in the open box and take a box or two for your mother."

Owen's face lit up. "That would be swell! See you tomorrow!"

March 19—In what is already being called the worst tornado in U.S. history, more than 600 people have died and some 13,000 were injured by a deadly twister that swept through Missouri, Illinois and Indiana yesterday. More than a mile in diameter, traveling at speeds surpassing 70 miles an hour, the tornado left razed buildings and torn-up railroad tracks in its wake.

"And I thought I had problems," Ruby told herself. Turning to the entertainment section, she gasped when she saw her name at the top of a short column on the bottom of the page.

Ruby No "Mrs. Grundy."
By Dick the Rounder
….This reporter has learned that prior to the accident, Ruby Adams was living at the Saint Francis Hotel, the same hotel where John Davis keeps a suite.

Ruby closed her eyes. Why now, after so many months? No one at the hotel had seemed interested in the couple's adjoining rooms. And it was old news. Why would anyone care?

"Herbert Choynski, their attorney, is full of dirty

tricks," Brennan had warned her. "We should expect anything."

—᙮᙮᙮—

Several nights later, Coffee Dan's was in full swing. The huge neon coffee cup outside the building seemed to pulsate with excitement. Downstairs, the piano player pounded out an extra-lively version of "Ain't We Got Fun." A layer of smoke hovered over the long rectangular cellar floor. There were about thirty wooden tables, all set with little wooden hammers. There were two ways to descend to the restaurant from street level: a highly polished slide and a stairway. Custom called for patrons to give every person who chose the slide "a hand." The pounding of the tiny mallets made an ear-splitting noise.

Rat-ta tat-tat, rat-ta-tat-tat. Rat-ta tat-tat, rat-ta-tat-tat.

"Here comes…Alice. Give her some hammering! Hullo, Alice!" the crowd yelled.

Rat-ta tat-tat, rat-ta-tat-tat.

Catcalls and hoots and hollers added to the din as a young girl slid into the room and onto a perfectly positioned scarlet pillow, custom-made in the shape of a coffee cup.

"Say, bartender, gimme an Orange Blossom," she hollered, giggling.

"I'll have a Gin Rickey," called her smartly dressed escort.

The bartender was serving a couple at the bar

drinking from oversize beige mugs. The overdressed woman wore a lot of makeup and the man seemed fidgety, kicking the brass rail as he purchased two packs of gum from the cigarette girl. Wearing a red saloon-style skirt and a jaunty pillbox hat held in place by the leather strap under her chin, Princess Margaret gave the bartender a wink and said, "I'll be right back. I need to refill my tray."

No one noticed when the door at the top of the stairs opened and four men, two police and two federal agents, hurried down into the speak. A shrill whistle pierced the smoky room as one of them called, "This is a raid! Stop where you are."

Thick coffee cups holding a variety of liquor dropped to the floor as the crowd fled through a back door or up the stairs. Cigarettes lay smoldering in ashtrays.

The whistle broke John Davis' concentration, and he looked up to see the red light above his door blinking. The hatcheck girl had been instructed to press the silent alarm if anything looking like trouble arose. He locked the ledger in the floor safe beneath his desk, then stood up and put on his jacket. The door to his office opened, and there stood a federal agent.

"What is this?"

"I have some bad news, Coffee Dan. Your establishment is being raided."

An hour later, Davis was sitting on a bunk in a cold cement cell at the Hall of Justice, awaiting his attorney. Hearing the thud of a man's heavy steps, he stood up and went to the barred door as a tall, broad figure came down the passageway.

"Good of you to come so soon, Brennan."

"I'm busy with an important case, but you seem critical to my client's well-being. Did they feed you?"

The closest café was an Italian restaurant around the corner, on the ground floor of a three-story apartment building. The handsome maître de had been about to close up, but he escorted the two to the back of the dining room and a table lit by a candle in a bulbous old wine bottle. Each ordered a bowl of minestrone soup.

"You know I've warned you about Colonel Choynski," Brennan said. "His nickname is 'the fighting colonel.' He advances, advances, and never retreats. I have a funny feeling that he was behind this."

"I assumed it was the McDonoughs. Word on the street is that they owe someone a favor."

Brennan raised a spoon of the minestrone to his lips. "Mmm, that's good. I'm curious, what else did you hear?"

"I didn't hear any specifics, why?"

"Must have been a pretty big favor. But there's no reason to think they weren't working together."

As Brennan sipped his soup, he wondered why Pete McDonough had been at the Strand the night of the accident. Hard to think it had been a coincidence, and that he didn't have anything to do with the accident or the missing sandbag.

He leaned forward and picked at the wax of the candle as it fell onto the red-checkered table-cloth. "McDonough got out of prison early six months ago."

"I heard. Coolidge pardoned him."

Brennan nodded. "I wonder if Coolidge owed him a favor."

The waiter cleared the soup bowls and returned with a plate of thinly sliced veal with capers and a platter of spaghetti with two huge meatballs.

Davis frowned and picked up his fork. "Counselor, don't get distracted by McDonough."

"I'm just wondering why his name keeps coming up, that's all," Brennan said.

After the meal, Davis paid the check and the two men walked out to the empty street. It was so quiet, you could hear the foghorns bellowing at ships somewhere in the distance.

"Listen," Davis told Brennan, "I have no beef with McDonough. That's not a fight I want. My business can handle the loss." He paused. "I need you to concentrate on Ruby and these schmucks who own the Strand."

At the Hall of Justice, Brennan took a set of keys from his pocket. "Can I offer you a lift?"

"Thanks. Can you take me back to the St. Francis Hotel? I want to clean up before heading over to the hospital first thing in the morning."

◆

Fourteen

The boardinghouse on Hayes Street had survived the 1906 earthquake. Not so the business of the family that owned the building, which had once been a large home. This part of the city had been saved from the fire that engulfed San Francisco after the quake, mostly due to the wide expanse of Van Ness Avenue. Basil might have found a room closer to the theater, but he liked the location, close to his favorite speakeasy.

"No girls in your room tonight, Basil!" warned Mrs. Sedgewick, the elderly woman who ran the place. Basil waved her off. She was a good soul, though a little nosy. Rosetta Sedgewick could tell something was bothering him. He hadn't been himself for months.

Basil tucked his handkerchief into his coat pocket and turned down Gough Street. All the streetcars heading up Market toward the city's westward expansion briefly drove thoughts of his deposition away. The city was changing so quickly, he thought, walking past two-story brick apartment buildings with retail shops on the ground floor.

The Swedish American Hall was an odd place for a speakeasy. The city's Swedish American Society had opened the place the year after the earthquake. It liked advertising the "old-world charm" of the restaurant in the basement, though Basil, as usual, was heading to the dim bar.

He had been raised in a religious family and been taught that drinking alcohol was a sin. That hadn't stopped him from taking a nip or two before a show at the Strand, but over the past seven months, he'd head to the Café Du Nord every chance he got, to drink Gin Rickeys and maybe meet some girls.

The only light in the windowless basement came from a single pendant lamp, hung from the pressed-tin ceiling over the bar, and a row of tapered candles at the far end of the room. Basil joined the other hard-working stiffs at the long mahogany bar and signaled the bearded bartender.

He lowered his head and stared at his hands glumly. Earlier that week, he'd gotten word from Charles Brennan, Ruby Adams' attorney, that he was to appear in court for a deposition. Basil did not know what that meant exactly, but he didn't like the way things were going. Despite assurances from Mr. Markowitz, this lawsuit was not going away. Knowing that he was responsible for the fly system, Basil was afraid Mr. Markowitz and his partner were going to blame everything on him. They were avoiding every request to meet and pushing him toward their loud-mouthed attorney.

At least he still had a job. Since the accident, Basil had been working in the Strand's third-floor projection room, where he changed out the movie reels and ran the projector. Gone were the gorgeous chorus girls he enjoyed flirting with, the colorful vaudeville shows and backstage drama. Now he was alone in a claustrophobic hundred-square-foot closet with a whirring machine and smelly celluloid film. His only work with the fly system was raising the grand curtain that hid the giant movie screen as an organist he never saw played an effervescent tune.

But things were changing around the theater. Bill Finck was gone, and there were new owners who talked about schools for theater managers. He'd seen a pamphlet that offered classes on how to sell a show and how to write stories for the press.

Thinking of the press made him think of the lawsuit. Like a cat who appears from nowhere, a woman pressed her breast into his shoulder. "Hello, blue eyes. Don't you smell good!"

"What are you doing for dinner, doll?" Basil asked.

"I'm dining with you."

"And after?"

The woman laughed as she followed Basil through the narrow entrance of the Viking Room.

—◁◊▷—

San Francisco City Hall was the most beautiful building Basil had ever seen. The blue-and-green iron work on the doors, which opened to an expansive rotunda with marble pillars on either side; the narrow arched windows below the ornamental dome; the sweeping central stairway; the elaborate ornamentation—it was far more impressive than any of the movie palaces he'd seen in San Francisco. The place took his breath away.

A slight, dark-haired woman startled Basil as he stood looking up the staircase, wondering where it led.

"Mr. Knoblock?"

"Yes, how did you know?"

"I'm here to escort you to your deposition."

"Is my attorney here?"

"Not yet."

Basil gripped his brown bowler tightly as he followed the woman into an elevator and up to the fourth floor, where the courtrooms were located. Department 13 was down a long corridor at the northwest corner of the building. The woman stopped at a door marked Jury Room, and they went in.

"Mr. Knoblock, hello, I'm Charles Brennan. Come." he said motioning to Knoblock to move forward. "You understand that you are here to give a deposition about events on the night of January 10, 1925. Is that correct?"

"Yes," Basil said.

Once seated, the stagehand placed his derby on the long table, looked about uneasily and asked about his attorney.

"The deposition cannot go forward without him," Brennan said with a conciliatory smile.

The interview would be recorded by a smartly dressed court reporter, sitting at the end of the table, already using her blue fountain pen to scribble on a stenographer's pad in shorthand. Brennan placed a newly sharpened pencil next to his own legal pad and several pages of questions, which he proceeded to study.

Basil dug in his pocket for his handkerchief as he considered what might transpire over the next hour or two. He replayed the accident in his mind, as he did every day. He had hurried backstage after fixing the radiator in the lobby. He sat down in front of the fly system. He unlocked the line set from the pin rail to lower the curtain that would hide the backdrop for the burglar sketch. His callused hands were gripping the rope during Ruby and Jack's second curtain call when he felt a slight hitch; gripping it again during Will's second curtain call, he'd suddenly felt it go slack. Once more, he felt his stomach drop in horror when he felt the stage floor shake, and he knew that something was terribly wrong. He turned around and saw the broken sandbag on the stage. He shuddered when he remembered seeing Miss Adams lying under it, covered in sand. Sweat broke out on his upper lip, and he wiped his face with the handkerchief. He wanted a drink. Since he couldn't pull out his flask, he took out a cigarette and lit it.

Just then, Colonel Herbert Choynski burst into the room, explaining that his chauffeur had struck a pedestrian en route from the financial district.

"Not much damage to the car, and minor bruises on the chap, as luck would have it," he announced. Turning to Charles Brennan, he said, "May I have a word with my client, counselor?"

"Of course. There's an office next door, as you already know."

In the little room, Choynski explained the situation to Basil.

"There's not much more we can do to fight this, my boy. You'll need to cooperate fully, answer all the questions to the best of your ability."

"Now listen, I told Bill Finck the equipment was getting old, I told him and told him, but no one did nothing."

"Everything will be all right. You must have faith, son!"

Basil held his derby tightly, rubbing the brim so hard with his thumb and forefinger, he was crushing the felt.

"Sir, this is not my fault. I did my job!" Listening patiently, Choynski brought his liver-spotted hands together as if he were praying. "I told Mr. Lesser the ropes were too old and we needed to change them out."

"Listen here. You have no proof of that, and it was your job to take care of the equipment. Wait, wait—" he interjected, as Basil started to speak. "I've been authorized to offer you ten thousand dollars, if you do exactly as I say. It'll be best for all of us."

Basil leaned back and glared at Choynski. He felt sick. "Go on."

A few minutes later, Basil straightened his tie and walked back into the conference room. Choynski notified the court reporter that they were ready to begin the deposition, and all returned to their seats. The room was oppressively stuffy. The court reporter asked if she should open a window. As she pushed the window outward, a police siren screamed in the distance.

Brennan cleared his throat and asked no one in particular, "Shall we begin?"

The court reporter nodded and swore in the witness.

"Mr. Knoblock," Brennan began, "what was your occupation on January 10, 1925?"

"Stagehand."

"And where were you working?"

"At the Strand Theater."

"So you were employed as a stagehand at the Strand Theater on January 10, 1925?"

"Yes, sir."

"Who hired you?"

"Mr. Markowitz."

"Do you recall when that was?"

"I believe it was…sometime in 1920."

"What were your duties?"

"Lots of things."

"Mr. Knoblock, please list your duties for the record."

Knoblock studied his hands before answering. "I helped with carpentry. I worked and, um, maintained the rigging system."

"Please explain the rigging system. Were you responsible for the…one minute," Brennan looked down at his notes, "I think you call it the fly system or fly-rigging system?"

"Yes."

"Please explain what the fly system is."

"It's the way we handle the curtains, the backdrops, sometimes the lights and even the sound."

He looked at the court reporter, scribbling quickly to capture his testimony. He hoped she knew what she was doing.

"Mr. Knoblock, you say it was your job to maintain the equipment. What was your routine when inspecting it?"

"I climbed up to the fly loft and made a physical inspection of the rope, the batten pulleys, and the pipes that hold the lift lines."

The court reporter held up her hand. "One moment."

Brennan took a breath. He had become so familiar with theater vernacular, he hadn't realized he might be moving too quickly. A moment later, the court reporter nodded.

"Prior to the incident that occurred on January 10," Brennan said, "when was the last time you inspected the fly system?"

"I...." He shut his eyes briefly and sighed. "I wasn't able to check the fly system that night. Right before the show, there was a problem with the radiator in the lobby that I needed to attend to. I don't really know when the last time was—maybe two or three days before."

The minutes ticked by as Brennan had him review all his actions on the night of January 10.

"Mr. Knoblock, after the sandbag fell, did you notice the rope?"

"Yes."

"And what did you find?"

Basil's eyes did not betray him. "I found it in good condition, sir."

The stagehand didn't have much going for him, but he was a good liar. The rope had to have rotted and frayed to break like that, and Walter, the stage-door attendant, had told Ruby as much. Unfortunately, no one had any idea how to reach him now.

"Mr. Knoblock, you say the rope that held the sandbag that fell was in good condition?"

"Yes, sir."

Brennan paused.

"Mr. Knoblock, if the equipment was in good condition, how do you suppose the sandbag fell?"

"I don't know."

"Weren't you curious?"

"There was a lot going on that night, sir."

"I see." Brennan paused. "One more question. Were you drinking alcohol on the night of the accident?"

Choynski objected to the question as irrelevant and immaterial.

"Fine, Mr. Choynski, we will note your objection. Now," Brennan said, turning back to Basil, "I have it from two witnesses that you were seen drinking from a flask on the night of January 10. So I'll ask again, Mr. Knoblock. Were you drinking on the night of the accident?"

"I may have had a swig or two before the show to keep warm, that's all."

Herbert Choynski slammed his briefcase shut. "If that's your last question, we are done here, gentlemen."

—⁓—

It took Choynski's secretary the better part of the afternoon to track down Moe Lesser and ask him to meet the Colonel that evening. At seven o'clock, Lesser rang the bell to the Choynski residence, in Pacific Heights. A butler dutifully opened the door, and he entered. The Colonel stood in the hallway in his uniform from the Spanish-American War. The buttons on the lower portion of the jacket were unbuttoned, allowing his stomach to protrude. As

Choynski ushered him into his study, Moe heard the metal from the Colonel's sword scrape and his leather boots squeak.

"Come in," Choynski gestured. "I've just been at a reunion of Battery B, First Battalion, over at the Presidio. Can I interest you in a nip of cognac?"

"That would be nice, Colonel."

They sat across from one another in soft leather chairs, a beautifully carved chess set on a little table between them, sipping cognac like liquid gold from crystal snifters. As always, the Colonel smoked a cigar he had shipped in from Cuba.

When he spoke, his dark eyes were fierce. "I think you should know there's a good chance that we'll lose the war. I'm afraid it was foolish to think otherwise."

"The war?"

"The case, man. I was using war as a metaphor." he said with some irritation.

"I see. How can you be so sure we're going to lose?"

"I've been an attorney for many years, son. We have a sympathetic judge, and we're going to trial. That's never good—the jury is likely to side with Ruby Adams and may award her a sizable judgment."

Lesser sat beside a Tiffany lamp, staring at the logs burning in the fireplace. It was late summer in San Francisco, which meant that outside, a wet fog blanketed everything. The mantle displayed several photographs of Choynski's daughter, who was studying something or other in Italy. There was a loud snap, and a log broke in two.

"Jurors are often soft-hearted, young man. Ruby is young and paralyzed through no fault of her own, no matter what I say in court. The chances of success with a jury are small, I'm afraid."

"But you said—"

Choynski took the cigar from his mouth. Lesser noticed that the uniform made him look and act younger.

"Listen, I found out at the deposition today that Knoblock had been drinking that night! He was under your employ! I brought you here to discuss how to proceed, not to discuss the merits of the claim or whatever I said earlier. You might well lose the case. What's important now is to hide your assets. You don't want the courts to latch onto your money, boy!"

Clearly, Lesser had not thought this far ahead. The Colonel leaned forward and took three chess pieces from the board.

"Now, hear me out. We'll need to issue a series of checks—for salaries, administrative costs, legal fees, that sort of thing—eliminating all funds in the company's bank account. We'll have to come up with the right figures, but it can be done. We'll move the money from the corporation's account," he said, placing a white pawn on the board next to a knight, "to individual accounts. It's important that you hide the money from the court."

He set a black queen on the table, then lay the white pawn and white knight on their sides, as if they had been taken by the queen. "The chorus girl cannot execute the judgment on anything you don't own!"

They spent the next hour discussing ways of distributing the money. The details grew in complexity. "Open an account in Paris....or perhaps Tokyo." Choynski was surprisingly well versed in banking matters. As a young man, he had worked at the Anglo & London Paris National Bank and been a student of international trade and financing, specifically with countries in Europe and Asia.

"I have many friends in the world of finance. And I can tell you, executing judgments against funds held in foreign banks is *not* easy."

"Very interesting," Moe said. "You've thought of everything, haven't you?" He grinned. "Well, I need to get Morris's buy-in on the plan."

"The sooner the better," Choynski declared. "We must do this before the trial. If Brennan gets wind that we're up to some cockamamie plan, he'll bring an injunction to keep us from transferring those assets."

As Lesser stood, he looked at the mantle again, and a photograph of Joe Choynski caught his eye. He hadn't seen him in years.

"How's your brother?"

"Fine. He's teaching boxing in Illinois."

Lesser nodded. "I'll call Morris tonight."

Lesser waited until his wife went to bed before telephoning his partner. He seemed to be expecting the call.

◆

Fifteen

arly the next morning, Morris Markowitz stood leaning over the kitchen sink eating a slice of Graham bread with butter. Juliette stood wordlessly by his side. He was too nervous to sit, and it took every ounce of his strength to finish eating the heavy bread. He could feel trouble. Selling the theater was supposed to bring a new beginning. After the trial, if there was a trial, he thought he might take Juliette on that trip to Japan she'd been talking about. Maybe buy a home in Los Angeles. But the call from Moe had scared him. *The Colonel thinks we are going to lose the case. We need to talk about our next steps.*

Morris took a sip of hot coffee. He couldn't stomach losing the case and having to pay half the judgment. Fifty thousand dollars was a sum he couldn't afford. He forced himself to take a deep breath. What with the recent trip to Europe, the new house in Sea Cliff, his investments in the stock market and a small production company, he was terribly overextended. He should have saved more, spent less, but he'd never dreamed of having to face anything like this.

Juliette asked gently, "Morris, can't you tell me what's wrong?" Morris had always been reluctant to talk about money with his wife. He liked buying her whatever she wanted and loved spending money on his family. And she'd never been interested in the movie business. But today, he saw no other option.

"It was madness to believe we could win this. That call from Moe last night—well, the Colonel thinks we're going to lose the case. He's the wrong attorney to be negotiating this."

Juliette chose her words carefully. "Darling, you had no other choice, it's what Moe Lesser wanted. Don't worry, we'll get through this. We have each other and our little girl. I'm sure the courts will let you pay the judgment in installments."

"Juliette, listen to me, I haven't worked since Paramount bought the theater, and the award could drain our savings." He reached for the black jacket draped over a chair. "I'll know more this afternoon." He gave her a distracted kiss and walked out the door.

And so the conspiracy to hide the assets of Moses Lesser and Morris Markowitz, as well as those of the New York & San Francisco Amusement Company, commenced. Morris made his way to the second floor of the Flood Building, above the Lesser Brothers Market. A huge freezer stood at the far end of the hallway; beside it, half a dozen handcarts. Morris heard men laughing as the door opened. One man was carrying a large bloody sack in a pair of large bloody hands. The smell made Morris gag, and he turned his head aside and hurried down the hall. He opened the dingy door marked OFFICE with relief.

Lesser and Choynski were already preparing the bank checks. "Good morning," Lesser said calmly, looking up from the company's check ledger.

"Morning, Morris," Choynski said affably. "I know you spoke with Moses last night, but it's my duty to make everything clear. In this kind of case— the jury must decide whether the defendants are liable or not. If the defendants are found liable, the jury then determines the damages, the amount the plaintiff should get for compensation. As you know, the plaintiffs are asking for a hundred and one thousand dollars. The jury could award that much or determine another amount, either lower or higher. It's up to them."

Morris forced himself to take a series of deep breaths. "Oh, God," he muttered.

"Let me continue."

"Go on," Morris said, sounding a little calmer. "I don't mind saying I can't afford to lose the money."

"Once a decision for damages is announced, the court can freeze your assets. I recommend that you protect your assets from Miss Adams and her lawyer, who can ask the court to help them get the money the jury awards her."

"We have a plan," Moe added, handing Morris a folder containing all the checks written on the company's bank account at Anglo and London Paris National Bank of San Francisco. "As of this morning, the amount deposited into the corporation's bank account stands at three hundred and eighty thousand dollars. We have two hundred and fifty thousand in Publix stock. We should sell the stock Monday morning, as soon as the markets open, and distribute the cash. In preparation for the dispersal of the account, we've prepared these checks."

Morris opened the folder and thumbed through the checks slowly. "Clever. What about the remainder of the money?"

"The rest of the money will be transferred to an account in Tokyo and used to pay salaries and past-due bills."

"So we're stripping the corporation of all its money."

"Yes. You don't want the money anywhere the courts can attach it," Choynski said. "Time is running out. As soon as Brennan gets wind that the theater has been sold, he'll ask the court for an injunction to freeze your assets."

Morris took the checks from the folder and laid them out on the desk. The numbers lit up

Markowitz's eyes. His initial investment made a handsome profit. Then briefly, he thought about Ruby. The poor girl was paralyzed, after all. It was a terrible thing to do to her—deceitful and low. He would have liked to give her something—but they were asking for so much! And she had John Davis to take care of her. He had a wife and child to think about. This would protect his assets and support the kind of life to which he and his family had become accustomed.

"Hand me the pen."

Choynski ran his arthritic hands over his mustache and grinned as Moe made a joke about signing like John Hancock, which meant his signature should be easily recognizable.

"There they are, gentlemen," Lesser said, gesturing at the checks. "First thing Monday, I'll go down to the Pacific Stock Exchange and sell the Publix stock, and then we can bury our treasure, like real pirates."

All three laughed. The apathy of the men in the little office was matched only by their greed.

"Perhaps we should celebrate," Moe said, gesturing toward several glasses on a side table. "I have some nice Russian vodka handy for just such an occasion." Though it was well before noon, his colleagues readily agreed to the suggestion.

Lesser went to the meat freezer and brought back a chilled bottle of vodka. As he poured three very large glasses, a conspiratorial smile crossed his lips.

Lifting his glass, he said cheerfully, "L'chayim!"

Choynski eyed the check in his hand as the men toasted. He would endorse it for attorney's fees and deposit the rest of the money into three bank accounts he had. One was an account for his daughter, at Wells Fargo Bank in San Francisco. If she married Mortimer Fleishhacker, Jr., theirs would be an expensive society wedding.

Morris Markowitz deposited one-third of his money in the Hollywood National Bank and asked for the rest in cash, which he placed in the vault in his home.

Moses Lesser endorsed his check and handed it to his bookkeeper at Lesser Brothers Market, asking him to "take care of it."

———

After all the delays, foot dragging, and outright refusal to produce documents, disingenuously claiming attorney-client privilege, the defense suddenly moved at a remarkable speed. The court was unaware that Colonel Choynski, fearing that news regarding the sale of the Strand would become public, had advised going to trial as soon as possible. He asked for a court date, and the trial was scheduled for the following month.

After her release from the hospital a few weeks earlier, Ruby was living with her brother and his wife, in a cozy wooden bungalow just outside the eastern entrance to Golden Gate Park. Brennan began preparing his client to testify on a foggy August afternoon. The two sat in the kitchen, Ruby in a wicker wheelchair beside the table, as gusts of wind rattled the windows. Atop the table sat two coffee cups, a plate of muffins, and a folder. In the folder were five items: a photograph of Ruby, an architectural rendering of the theater, a pencil sketch of the courtroom, and two newspaper clippings.

"Where shall we start?" Ruby asked as she rearranged the purple shawl draped over her legs. She had gained several pounds since leaving the hospital, and Brennan noticed she looked stronger as well, although she was still terribly pale.

"The courtroom," Brennan replied. "Appearing in court is not unlike being onstage. This is your audience," he continued, holding up the pencil sketch and pointing to the jury box and the judge's bench. "The most important members of the audience are Judge Deasy and the jury—no one else in the courtroom matters, though I assume it will be filled with spectators."

"Where will the men I am suing sit?"

"Over here," he pointed to a narrow rectangle opposite the judge. On it were three Xs, which Brennan told her represented the plaintiffs and their lawyer. "But you do not have to see or look at them."

After twenty minutes of discussing her testimony and what Choynski might ask during cross-examination, she grew frustrated. "You want me to face the court with a smile, the way I used to face a theater crowd. I know a thing or two about performing, but I don't feel gay or have the pep I had when I...." Her voice trailed off. "What do I care about the money, if only I could walk again?"

Brennan shook his head as he saw the tears in her eyes. "Listen, as your attorney, I must tell you not to say that to anyone. Not to your family, not to the reporters, and especially not in the courtroom. I'm serious."

She recoiled and then said, "I understand. I will play it straight, or as straight as I can from a wheelchair."

Brennan sighed and warned her again about Choynski's histrionics and bullying. "Understand, too, that Herbert Choynski will try anything to increase his chances of winning this case! The man once shot off a gun in the middle of a courtroom to make a point," he said, handing her a news clipping. "Here, in this article, he calls the prosecuting attorney a coward. While I believe Judge Deasy will do his best to contain his antics, we must be ready for anything."

They worked through dinner on the line of questioning Brennan had prepared. Ruby understood her testimony was their best weapon, and, led by Brennan's gentle questions, she was prepared to deliver a compelling story. Brennan was amazed at how Ruby kept going, hour after hour.

But eventually, her strength faded, and she needed to leave the wheelchair and lie down.

They practiced the questions and answers until Brennan felt Ruby was ready. She never sounded as if she had memorized lines, and she never answered the same way twice. Her anger at the theater owners was channeled into a desire to make sure her responses conveyed the defendants' negligence. Brennan began to hope for a favorable outcome and judgment.

But all the preparation and, no doubt, nerves about the trial took a toll. Just days before the trial was set to begin, Brennan got a call from Ruby's doctor. He was not saying she could not testify, he told Brennan quickly, although he wished he could forbid it. But she was not strong enough to do so from a wheelchair.

Brennan immediately called Judge Deasy's office and asked if Ruby could testify from a stretcher.

———

At the start of September, farmers in the Central Valley were busy preparing fruit for the drying season. Basil Knoblock and a friend drove up to Sacramento to earn some extra money cutting and laying sliced apricots and apples out on tables for drying. The two men enjoyed the mindless work and used the weekend trip to get away from city life and swim in the American River. All the rain earlier in the year had brought a healthy snowpack, and the river was still running high in September.

It did not take long for Basil and his friend to locate the local speakeasy in Folsom, a town that catered to the gold miners in the area. That Sunday, after finishing a few drinks, Basil's pal handed over the key to his automobile. "We better get going. Back to the big city, my friend. Start her up. I'm going to see a man about a horse." Basil took the key as he laughed heartily.

By then, it was approaching six o'clock. Basil, wearing a thin sleeveless undershirt and a pair of baggy pants, emerged from the speakeasy into the warm September air. He heard the cicadas chirping as he opened the Tin Lizzy's door. Basil paused and stared at the road ahead. He wasn't in much better shape than his friend, but the street lay empty and quiet, no one in sight. And he did like to drive.

He got in and advanced the spark until the engine rattled and then ran smooth. He released the handbrake lever and depressed the clutch, and the engine sprang to life. As his foot pressed on the accelerator, he turned the steering wheel and did a series of circles in the middle of the road, laughing his head off. That's when a policeman drove by.

"Good afternoon, officer," Basil said. "Is there a problem?" This was his friend's motorcar, he explained, and he was only "warming her up." He ignored requests to walk for the police officer and finally announced he had to get back to San Francisco that night for a very important court date.

"*D'joo* know Ruuuby Adams? I'm a witness in her trial," he slurred.

"Not my problem, pal. Let's take a little walk."

"Where's my friend? He'll tell you." Basil was still talking as the policeman put him in handcuffs and shoved him down the street to the jail. The officer turned, but he didn't see anyone.

The next day, Brennan received word from the defense that Basil Knoblock had been detained by the Folsom police on a drunken-driving charge and would not be present at the trial.

◆

Sixteen

I n an era when San Francisco was notorious for cozy relationships among politicians, unions, and the courts, the Superior Court of the State of California, in and for the City and County of San Francisco, sat on a top floor of San Francisco's City Hall, a proud symbol of judicial oversight.

On September 7, Honorable Daniel C. Deasy exited his chambers in his long black robe. His long fingers grasped the paneled door that led to the District 13 courtroom. The courtroom's bailiff, who had been sampling the Graham bread freshly baked by a clerk's wife, rushed to his assistance.

"I'll get that, Your Honor," he said, wiping crumbs from his lips and fingers.

The judge withdrew his hand. The law was full of ritual. He should have waited and allowed the bailiff to open the courtroom door and announce him. He stepped back and then slipped through the door.

"All rise," the bailiff boomed. The tall, popular Irish-Catholic judge climbed the three steps to the gleaming raised oak bench, took his seat in the high-backed leather chair, and gazed out at the courtroom.

Judge Deasy had a long record on the bench and was considered a careful, smart, and thorough jurist. He had graduated at the top of his class at Boalt Hall, the law school at UC Berkeley, and had won praise from lawyers who appeared before him and judges who served with him. But he knew all that could change, at least in the public eye, if he didn't get this highly publicized case right. He was very aware of Choynski and his courtroom antics.

The judge had an easy charm about him as he addressed the court, especially those who had been called to jury duty. He made a brief statement about the case and what was expected from the jurors.

During *voir dire*, the potential jurors sat nervously waiting to be called to the jury box. Many could ill afford to be there. Women had been allowed to serve on juries in California since 1917 but were often excused after pleading hardship; they needed to stay home with their children or work to put food on the table. All the potential jurors in Judge Deasy's courtroom that day were anxious to serve in the Ruby Adams case.

The two attorneys were a contrast in styles: Brennan, mild-mannered, friendly, and thoughtful; Choynski, brash and thoughtless. The defense rejected many potential jurors due to their familiarity with the accident or the plaintiff. Choynski dismissed a middle-aged woman who had seen Ruby perform at the Strand, and another because she was taking care of her sick mother. He summarily dismissed one man who stated he'd be suspicious if a defendant did not testify. Finally, nine men and three women were seated and sworn in. Brennan was pleased with the jury members and turned to his law partner. "Choynski's manner doesn't seem to impress the jury, Harold. I'm feeling very good about how that went." Harold Faulkner nodded as Judge Deasy adjourned court for that day. All the attorneys rushed back to their offices to make their final preparations for the trial.

On Tuesday, September 8, as a batch of crows cawed sharply outside the walls of the courtroom, the officers of the New York & San Francisco Amusement Company, Moses Lesser and Morris Markowitz, dutifully filed into the courtroom with their attorney and sat down at the defense table. Only the plaintiff's attorneys noticed that Basil Knoblock, also named as a defendant, was not in the room.

The trial was an opportunity for the matrons of Pacific Heights, for Peninsula heiresses and their debutante daughters, to learn about the inner workings of the court and the vaudeville stage. The hallway outside the courtroom was filled with expensively dressed women, but they were outnumbered by reporters from all the local news outlets, as well as from newspapers as far away as Los Angeles and Seattle. The reporters and society women were issued thick blue cards allowing them ADMISSION. As the press and spectators entered Room 435, they handed their cards to the bailiff and took their seats.

"Goodness me, this is the first time I've been in a courtroom," one lavishly perfumed woman said to the woman beside her. "I have to say, these wooden chairs are very uncomfortable."

The other woman nodded. "Yes, but I had to come and see for myself. This story is so tragic. Poor soul. Oh, is that Coffee Dan over there?" she asked, pointing to someone in the first row of spectators, just behind the plaintiff's lawyers.

"I think it is."

"My, he's an elegant-looking man. They say he still wants to marry her."

Someone said the tall blond man in the back row was from a Hollywood paper. The most intriguing spectator was a dark-haired, Mediterranean-looking man whom one of the women had overheard speaking with a Greek accent, she was sure. Only

Ruby knew that she was a favorite of a certain Seattle shipping baron.

The atmosphere in the courtroom was electric, as if all were awaiting the curtain rising on a particularly exciting show—which, to most of the spectators, it was. The court reporter slipped into the room just before the bailiff announced, "All rise. The court is now in session. We will proceed with the case of Ruby Adams vs. the New York & San Francisco Amusement Company, Messrs. Lesser, Markowitz, and Knoblock. The Honorable Judge Daniel C. Deasy is presiding."

Judge Deasy, recently reelected to the Superior Court by the people of San Francisco, sat down at the bench and nodded. By this time, daily headlines had made the case the talk of the town, and every seat in the courtroom was filled. Deasy and his wife had both noted how invitations from friends, acquaintances, and people they barely knew had increased as soon as the public learned that he would be presiding over the case. He picked up his spectacles and opened a ledger and then struck the bench with his gavel.

At the plaintiff's table, Charles Brennan and Harold Faulkner sat on each side of an empty chair, representing the plaintiff, Ruby Adams.

Brennan's fitted brown suit had been carefully tailored without padded shoulders, to make his large frame appear smaller. He did not want to appear to tower over the witnesses or the jury. He tightened the knot of a new purple silk tie with diagonal stripes as he stood to address the court. The plaintiff must prove the defendants are liable under the law, and he had been up late into the night going over his opening statement.

"Good morning, ladies and gentlemen. My name is Charles Brennan, and I represent the plaintiff, Miss Ruby Adams. Miss Adams regrets that she cannot be here for my opening statement. Her transportation here requires special arrangements, due to the paralyzing injuries she sustained on January 10, 1925, while backstage at the Strand Theater. However, Miss Adams will be here later this morning."

Brennan enjoyed the drama of presenting a case to a jury. He had a good grasp of the English language and an intelligence that allowed him to assess situations quickly, to think on his feet. What's more, he understood that juries tended to like him. His clerks had overheard comments such as "What a decent, handsome man." Despite his affable, low-key manner, there was a coolness about Brennan that made it difficult for opposing attorneys to know what he was thinking—a poker face, they called it.

"As Judge Deasy has told you, the plaintiff has the burden of proof. We will prove without a doubt that Miss Adams was harmed due to the negligence of the New York & San Francisco Amusement Company and Messrs. Lesser and Markowitz, seated over there," pointing to the defense table. "This isn't a complex case. This is a case about a company that cut corners to generate more profits and, in so doing, put the lives and safety of hardworking performers in jeopardy.

"In addition to motion pictures, the company booked vaudeville shows and talent into the Strand Theater. The New York & San Francisco Amusement Company, which owns and operates the Strand Theater, had contracted with the Will King Follies to perform in their theater for six weeks. Ruby—Miss Adams—was a performer, an employee of the Will King Follies. As an employee, Miss Adams would need to be in the theater, and specifically in the wing near the stage where the injury occurred.

"As owners and directors of the New York & San Francisco Amusement Company, Messrs. Lesser and Markowitz managed the premises and exercised control over all the equipment inside the theater. It was their duty to maintain the theater's equipment in good working order. Because Messrs. Lesser and Markowitz breached their duty to maintain the equipment, they put the performers—and theatergoers—at risk, all the while taking in tickets and making a profit.

"During the course of this trial, you will learn how Miss Adams was struck by a three-hundred-pound sandbag that fell from the rafters of the theater. This is undisputed. The defendant Basil Knoblock will tell you that after the accident, he found the rope that suspended the sandbag in good working order. But you will not be able to decide that for yourselves. We will not be able to show you that evidence, because that evidence is missing. It is missing because the defendants discarded that evidence. I ask you, if the rope was in good working order, why would they discard it? There can be only one reason. The defendants neglected to keep the equipment in the theater in good condition; the sandbag broke and fell for this reason. Why else would they discard such critical evidence?"

Brennan paused and looked at the jury.

"Miss Adams's injuries from the heavy sandbag required surgery, and then a lengthy stay, a stay of eight long months, in St. Francis Hospital. The voluminous medical testimony may take up a day in itself. You will hear that Miss Adams is now and will be a helpless invalid for the rest of her life. She has suffered serious, lifelong effects from the injuries she sustained at the Strand that evening, when a damaged sandbag fell on her spine. Those are the facts." Brennan looked at each member of the jury. "Thank you."

The jury's eyes fell upon Markowitz, Lesser, and their lawyer. All knew it was time for the defense attorney's opening statement.

"Mr. Choynski," Judge Deasy said.

Choynski, dressed in a new custom-made suit and muted gray tie, stood and turned to the jury box. "Good morning, ladies and gentlemen of the jury. My name is Herbert Choynski, and it is my privilege to represent Messrs. Lesser, Markowitz, and Knoblock in this case before you today. You have heard the plaintiff's lawyer explain what he hopes to prove in this case, but the plaintiff's attorney did not tell you all of the facts. The plaintiff claims that my clients are responsible for her accident. In fact, it is the plaintiff herself who is responsible, because she was in a part of the theater which is known to be dangerous."

Brennan looked over to see how the jury was taking this. Was Choynski's defense about shifting the blame from his clients to the plaintiff? Was he really claiming that Ruby, a performer, should never have been standing in the wing? He and Faulkner glanced at each other, silently laughing at the preposterous legal strategy.

Choynski continued, "The plaintiff's attorney has told you the sandbag was purposely discarded to hide its condition, yet there is not one witness who saw this evidence being discarded. In fact, one of the defendants will state, under oath, that he inspected the bag after the accident and it was in good working order. I beg you to keep an open mind and listen to all the facts, and then return a verdict of not guilty. Thank you."

Choynski sat down and leaned over his notes as Judge Deasy picked up his gavel. "The court will take a twenty-minute recess."

As Choynski's opening remarks wound down, a green-and-cream-colored ambulance had turned onto Grove Street and cautiously backed in next to an ice truck at the City Hall loading dock. Brennan and Faulkner had decided to bring Ruby in for her testimony only. She would arrive after a brief morning recess and testify through lunch, if necessary.

Two mailroom clerks with broad shoulders were dispatched to help transport her from the loading dock up to the fourth-floor courtroom.

Dressed in a white cotton nightgown and wrapped securely in white sheets, Ruby was lifted from the ambulance onto a hospital carriage. A nurse checked her position and straightened the sheets. The athletic-looking ambulance driver quickly cinched the leather buckles, pulled back a lever, and motioned to the two men.

As the carriage moved forward, her brother took hold of a milky-white arm and walked alongside Ruby, encouraging her. "Chin up," he said heartily. "You've faced the public many times before."

"But this is the first time I'm unable to do it with a smile." As a gentle breeze briefly touched her cheek, Ruby made no further anxious comments.

The clattering carriage rolled down a cement ramp and into the City Hall basement. The men rolled the carriage past the dumbwaiter and some time-card slots on the wall next to a dirty freight elevator and guided it inside.

Two minutes later, the metal gates of the elevator opened onto an unruly crowd of reporters. Ann Durham, the nurse, shouted, "Back away, please, and let us through!" as the metal gates snapped shut behind them. The carriage rolled down the long hallway as murmurs and shouts erupted from the spectators. The reporters and the bailiff quickly put out their cigarettes and rushed back into the courtroom.

"The court calls Ruby Adams," the bailiff announced as a hush fell over the room.

Except for the defendants, everyone turned toward the back of the room and watched as Ruby Adams came through the door on a stretcher, accompanied by her nurse. Choynski removed his reading glasses and inspected the lenses as he realized the impression the plaintiff was making as the carriage rolled into the courtroom. With a nurse yet! Brennan's office had requested that she give her testimony from a stretcher, Choynski recalled, but he hadn't given it much thought.

Morris Markowitz leaned toward Moe Lesser and whispered urgently, "This isn't what we need." Moe recoiled at the smell of coffee and cigarettes on Morris's breath. He could feel his eye twitching as the stretcher reached the witness stand. His wife had been worried about a scene such as this and had warned Moe that morning to look humble and not to be brash.

Inside the courtroom, Ruby could hear a buzz

erupt among the crowd, she smiled. Judge Deasy's gavel fell. "Order in the court!"

Ruby lay parallel to the witness stand, facing the jury, in a sea of white sheets. It felt familiar in a way, like being onstage, but at the same time, everything seemed unreal. If only she were dreaming this! But hearing the murmurs in the crowd, feeling its attention brought solitude she may have been gone from the public's view, but she had not been forgotten.

Charles Brennan was soon at her side. He gave her a small smile and whispered, "You're on, Miss Adams."

Ruby nodded and then winked.

A blue jay screeching repeatedly outside the courtroom made it difficult to hear her testimony.

"Miss Adams, did you have a contract with Will King to perform with the Will King Follies?" Brennan asked.

"Yes, I did."

"How long was the contract?"

"For six months."

"When did the contract expire?"

"In March."

"What were your plans after the contract expired? Were you going to renew it?"

"Will wanted me to, but I had already signed a contract with a motion picture company in Los Angeles."

A buzz began in the courtroom.

"What is the name of that company?"

"Famous Players-Lasky."

"Is that a big company?" The blond man from the Los Angeles paper made a harrumphing sound.

"Order in the court," Deasy demanded.

"Yes. That's what I'm told."

"Famous Players-Lasky is one of the bigger production companies, is it not?"

Choynski stood. "Objection, Your Honor, irrelevant and repetitive."

"Sustained."

By now, the noise among the spectators was irritating Judge Deasy, especially with the bird outside doing all that screeching. "Order," he called, banging his gavel.

Brennan turned to his next line of inquiry. He withdrew two photographs from a folder and handed them to Ruby.

"Can you identify these photographs?" Both showed her dressed in a pinstripe suit with fox pelts draped around her shoulders.

"Yes, those are photographs of me taken in December 1924."

The photos were entered into court as Exhibits One and Two and handed to the jury to view. Choynski glanced at his clients and whispered something. As Brennan was handing the photographs to the bailiff, Choynski said, "Judge, could the plaintiff speak up, please?"

Brennan looked at Choynski and then back at his client and encouraged her to speak louder, suggesting the courtroom acoustics were not up to

snuff compared with a first-rate theater. This brought a nervous laugh from the jury.

"Miss Adams, were you performing at the Strand Theater on the night of January 10 of this year?"

"I was, yes."

"And where were you at the time of the accident?"

"I was standing in the right wing of the theater."

"And at this time, was Will King still performing onstage?"

"Yes, he was finishing his sketch and then he took a curtain call."

"And at that time, what did you do?"

"Just before going on the stage, we've been taught to check our costume one last time. There's a mirror there for that purpose." Ruby's throat was dry, and she swallowed. "I noticed my dance slipper had come undone, and I stooped over to refasten it. And then...."

"And then?" Brennan asked gently.

"And then I...." The jury saw the stretcher began to shake, and some of them frowned. There was a faint cry, then a prolonged silence and sudden stillness.

"She's fainted!" the court reporter cried.

"Oh, God," Markowitz muttered.

A juror shouted, "Do something!"

The nurse had already stepped forward and was beckoning a physician sitting among the spectators. Judge Deasy ordered the jury to be removed from the courtroom *immediately.*

As restoratives were administered to the plaintiff, one could hear a few moans in the courtroom, and many women brought lace-trimmed handkerchiefs to their eyes.

By then, it was twelve o'clock, which meant that San Franciscans, who were always early to rise, were due to take lunch. Once the jury returned to the courtroom, Judge Deasy swiftly adjourned for a lunch break.

An hour and an half later, the defense began its cross-examination of the witness. Herbert

Choynski put the cap on his fine gold pen as he stood and approached Ruby's stretcher. Ruby looked composed as he looked down at her, trying to appear sympathetic.

"Miss Adams, it has been nine months since your injury, is that correct?"

"Yes."

"And you say you were standing in the right wing of the stage when that occurred, is that correct?

"Yes."

"The fly system, the system responsible for controlling the curtains and backdrops, is also in the right wing, is that not correct?"

"Yes, that's correct."

"You were standing near the fly system, is that correct?"

"Yes, it's pretty cramped—"

"And the fly system is responsible for controlling the curtains and backdrops?"

"Yes, I believe we already agreed on that."

"It's a formidable piece of equipment, is it not?"

"Yes, it is."

"You said that Will King was still on stage, isn't that correct?"

"Yes."

"Well, if Mr. King was still on stage, shouldn't you have remained in your dressing room until summoned by the call boy?" Choynski's voice was suddenly loud and harsh. "You should not have been in the vicinity of the fly system, isn't that true?"

Ruby squeezed the rabbit's foot a friend had given her and said to herself, "You S.O.B."

Brennan rose to his feet. "Objection! Your Honor, Mr. Choynski is badgering my client. He must wait for her to answer the question before he asks another."

Judge Deasy replied, "Objection sustained! Mr. Choynski, please refrain from these compound questions, and there's no need to shout."

Choynski backed away from the stretcher and looked down at his arthritic hands. "Very well. Miss Adams, isn't it true that you should have remained in your dressing room until the call boy summoned you?"

She gathered her strength, and her voice carried across the room, "No, it is not true. Will King took another curtain call and delayed my entrance."

"Your Honor, this is not a feasible line of questioning," Brennan interjected. "Miss Adams was to be onstage in a matter of seconds. And the dressing rooms are downstairs."

"Sustained."

Choynski finished his cross-examination at three o'clock, and Brennan approached the stretcher for his redirect questioning.

"How are you doing, Miss Adams?"

"Yes," Judge Deasy added. "Do you need a break?"

"No, thank you, Your Honor. I'm fine," Ruby

said, looking up at her lawyer. Brennan winked.

"Miss Adams, how many times, during a Will King Follies performance, would a performer walk by or in front of the fly system?"

"Oh, half-dozen—possibly five or six times a night, depending on how many times you performed and how many curtain calls you took. There was no way to avoid it."

"Thank you, Miss Adams," Brennan smiled, squeezing her hand. "You are dismissed."

The bailiff lifted his head and looked at the judge. When Judge Deasy nodded, he brought in the two mailroom clerks, who walked over to the carrier and carefully glided it across the room to the door. People rose spontaneously, and someone said, "We are praying for you, Ruby." Then she heard another faint voice. "God bless you, Butterfly." Someone began clapping timidly, but soon others joined in, and the applause erupted. Judge Deasy was about to pick up his gavel but instead addressed the jury.

"Ladies and gentlemen of the jury, I must remind you not to read anything about this case in the press or to talk about it with anyone. Court is adjourned for the day. We will start tomorrow at ten a.m. sharp."

San Francisco Call-Bulletin
**Stage Beauty Goes to Court on Stretcher
Cripple for Life, Injured Girl
Testifies in Her Action for Damages.**

"... in the day's proceedings, the attorneys clashed: the defense contending that Miss Adams had no right to be at the spot where the sand bag fell, on the theory that she should have remained in her dressing room until summoned by the call boy."

◆

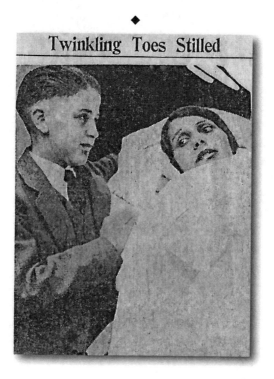

Twinkling Toes Stilled

Seventeen

The next day was uncomfortably warm, but by early afternoon, the wind had picked up, and the leaves of the sycamore trees around City Hall swirled chaotically in all directions. After lunch, at the court's order, the jury, judge, attorneys, and defendants were ushered outside and transported to the Strand Theater, five blocks away.

The men in the jury held onto their hats as they assembled outside the theater and gazed up at the marquee. The theater was showing *Wild Wild Susan*, starring Bebe Daniels and Rod La Rocque. An observant juror noticed, on one of the colorful posters out front, that it was a Paramount film produced by Jesse Lasky. The plaintiff's lawyer hadn't been allowed, he supposed, to ask what Ruby had contracted to do with Famous Players-Lasky, but he had to think that if she hadn't been injured, she'd be making a movie in Hollywood right now.

The jurors were heading backstage, to see for themselves the fly system responsible for raising and lowering the curtains and scenic backdrops. They were going to view its position in relation to where Ruby had been standing when the sandbag fell. Since that sandbag was not in evidence, they were going to view a similar sandbag.

"Shall we start the tour?" asked the polite young stage manager, in a crisp white shirt, black pants, and black bowtie. Brennan recognized Jeffrey Asher, surprised he still had a job. He wondered what had become of the unpleasant pockmarked fellow who had appeared to be Asher's boss.

The twelve jurors, two alternates, judge, bailiff, two defendants, defense attorney, Brennan, and Faulkner were ushered through a side door. All the jurors were excited to see the inner workings of a theater. The bailiff managed to keep the defendants and the attorneys away from the judge, jury members, and alternates, all of whom were looking around curiously. The backstage had been cleverly rearranged, Brennan noted, to avoid the impression of disorder. Looking down at some notes on a clipboard, Asher told the group that this was how the theater looked during a vaudeville production.

He showed them the monstrous fly system, including the cleats that secured the well-used ropes attached to about half a dozen sandbags that hung from the rafters. What they did not see was the sandbag that had fallen on Ruby. Brennan's voice rang in at least one juror's head. "If the sandbag was in good condition, why was it discarded?"

Finally, Asher sat down in front of the fly system and showed them how it worked. The judge and jury members' eyes were fixed on the pulley system as he worked. It was an impressive demonstration. All that was missing was a three-hundred-pound sandbag catapulting to the stage.

Asher then led them past what he called the prompt corner to the mirror in which Ruby had taken a final look at her costume. Toward the back of the right wing area was a stairway that led, he told them, to the dressing rooms. The jury could see that the mirror was located within a narrow passageway to the stage not far from the fly system. It seemed a dangerously cramped design.

Eyes wandered toward the defendants and their counsel. Markowitz and Lesser said nothing to each other or anyone else, and kept their heads down. Some thought they looked very uncomfortable. Brennan later described the mood backstage as tense.

The next morning, after Judge Deasy took the bench, he cleaned his spectacles and seemed to fall into a thoughtful silence. A minute passed before he opened the leather-bound ledger in front of him and called the court to order.

Brennan glanced up at the court clerk and told him his next witness was Will King. The bailiff went out to the hallway and quickly reentered the room, announcing, "The plaintiff calls Will M. King."

The Pacific Heights matrons watched with interest as a short, compact man with wiry brown hair and heavy eyebrows entered the courtroom, buttoning his coat. He gave the court clerk a perfunctory nod and was sworn in.

Charles Brennan stood up as King sat down in the witness box. "Good day, sir. Please state your name for the record."

"William Michael King."

"And please state your occupation."

"Vaudeville producer."

"Mr. King, you employed Ruby Adams and others in your musical performances with the Will King Follies, did you not?"

"Yes, I did."

"And your company was performing at the Strand Theater on the night of January 10, is that right?"

"Yes."

"Is the Will King Follies still performing at the Strand?"

"Well, we had a six-week contract, but we did not complete it."

"Why's that?"

"We were let go."

"Why?"

"Mr. Markowitz said we weren't pulling in the ticket receipts anymore."

Brennan paused.

"And do you know why not?"

"When Miss Adams was injured, our ticket sales fell. Many in the cast thought the theater was hoodoo—" Noting Brennan's questioning look, he added, "you know, jinxed, and maybe people who would have come to see the show did, too."

"Objection, speculation," Choynski bellowed.

"Sustained."

"Mr. King, is the Will King Follies performing elsewhere now?"

"No, sir. It was getting harder and harder to find work even before the sandbag fell on Ruby."

"And what are the members of your company doing now?"

"Some have found work, others have not."

"And you, Mr. King, are you working?"

"I've managed. I've got some work writing scripts for some of the movie companies."

"I see."

King verified that all the players in his company would have had to pass the spot where Ruby had been standing, on their way on and off the stage from the right wing. He noted that the bag had fallen so heavily, its metal rings injured a performer who'd been standing nearby.

"Mr. King, how talented was Miss Adams?"

"Objection, calls for speculation," Choynski said.

"I will allow. Overruled."

"She was a natural. She had *it*—that special something you can't describe but know when you see it. Everyone wants to hire a performer like that. When she sings, people think she's singing right to them. She has something special," King added, choking up. "I couldn't replace her," he finished, wiping his eyes.

"Objection!" Choynski said stridently. "These are nothing more than the witness' opinions."

"Overruled," Judge Deasy repeated. "Mr. King is a professional entertainer, and it's fitting to know his reasons for hiring Miss Adams. I will allow, Mr. Choynski."

Retreating to the plaintiffs table, Brennan picked up a piece of paper. "Mr. King, my records show," he began, looking at the paper, "that you paid over fifteen hundred dollars for Miss Adams's initial medical expenses. Is this true?"

"Yes."

"Why would you pay for her medical expenses?"

"It was a gift. I didn't want her to worry."

"Mr. King, you mentioned earlier that someone else was injured that night. What were her injuries?"

"Objection! This question is irrelevant to the case before us," Choynski declared.

"Sustained."

The point had been made, however. That's all Brennan wanted.

"No further questions, Your Honor."

"Mr. Choynski, do you have any questions for this witness?"

"Yes, I do, Your Honor. Mr. King, you hold a grudge against Mr. Markowitz, isn't that right?"

"Not particularly, no."

"But didn't you say Mr. Markowitz fired you?"

"Yes."

"Because your ticket sales fell by over sixty-five percent, didn't they?"

"Yes," King replied with a frown.

Juror number three looked at King as if surprised by this admission.

"Thank you. No further questions, Your Honor."

"The plaintiff calls Doctor Milton Lennon."

A distinguished gray-haired gentleman walked to the witness stand. Neatly dressed in a navy blue suit and maroon polka-dot tie, the surgeon made a striking figure. The Pacific Heights matrons later agreed he was a fine-looking man.

"Doctor Lennon, were you on duty at the Saint Francis Hospital on the night of January 10?" Brennan asked.

"Yes, I was."

"Can you tell us what occurred from your perspective on the night in question?"

The courtroom was still.

"After someone at the theater called the hospital, I was immediately dispatched, with an assistant, in an ambulance."

"When you arrived at the theater, what did you find? Let me rephrase that. Did you evaluate Miss Adams?"

"Yes, of course."

"Upon your evaluation, what did you find?"

"I found swelling, lacerations, and contusions on eighty percent of her body. She had a faint pulse, and her breathing was labored."

"Had you ever seen injuries like those sustained by Miss Adams?"

"Yes, once, after the earthquake. I was a resident then, and I examined a woman who had a brick chimney fall on her."

"And these types of injuries, what are they usually the result of?"

"A heavy blow to the body. We call it blunt-force trauma."

"Thank you, doctor. Now, what happened after you examined Miss Adams?"

"I felt the best course of action was to remove her to the hospital as quickly as possible."

"Why is that?"

"I was fearful that her ribs were broken and that a fragment of a rib could cause damage to a major organ. And Miss Adams was experiencing shortness of breath. I felt we needed to provide supplemental oxygen."

Brennan didn't respond immediately, letting the jury take this in.

"Then what did you do?"

"We immobilized her so that when we moved her, we wouldn't incur more damage."

"I see," Brennan said as he walked back to the plaintiffs table. "Dr. Lennon, is this an x-ray of the plaintiff, Miss Ruby Adams?" he asked as he lay an x-ray on the witness-stand railing.

Dr. Lennon lifted the x-ray to the light. "Yes, it is."

"When was it taken?"

"On the night of January 10, 1925."

"Your Honor, we ask the court to mark these as Exhibits." Brennan handed several x-rays to the court clerk, who marked them as evidence before Brennan brought them back to the witness stand.

"Doctor, please describe to the jury what these x-rays show."

"This x-ray indicates that the patient suffered a major trauma. The two lumbar vertebrae, L-four and L-five, were irreparably damaged, as well as the vertebra S-one. This x-ray here shows that three ribs were shattered and the right lung punctured, as I had feared."

"Now, what do the L-four, L-five, and S-one vertebrae do?" Brennan asked.

"The five lumbar vertebrae are between the rib cage and the pelvis. L-four and L-five are the biggest vertebrae in the spine and support the torso. The S-one vertebra enables rotation—that is, it allows the pelvis considerable rotation, so that we can run, walk, and....dance."

"Now Doctor, did Miss Adams require surgery?"

"We repaired her lung, using a tube, and immobilized the spine using a body cast. As I say, the three vertebrae were irreparably damaged, but she needed time to heal."

"Doctor, what treatments has the plaintiff received as a result of the injuries sustained on January 10?"

Holding the x-rays in his hands, Brennan looked over at the jury. They were leaning forward, listening intently. He thought about the information they were hearing for the first time. They had to find it distressing.

"For several months, Miss Adams was in a plaster body cast. That is to say, we replaced the body cast every two weeks, after removing it so that we could test her lower reflexes. Each time, we found them unresponsive to pain stimulus."

Brennan watched juror number three flinch. Then he asked his final question. "What is Miss Adams's prognosis?"

The courtroom seemed to grow even quieter. "Miss Adams will be paralyzed from the waist down for the rest of her life. At some point, she will need twenty-four-hour care."

"Can you tell us roughly how long Miss Adams will live?"

"Oh, she is healthy. While she will never be able to walk, if she remains in good health she could live to the average expectancy for a woman."

"And what would that be?"

"Seventy years."

"Objection! Speculation."

"Overruled, Mr. Choynski. Dr. Lennon is an expert witness."

"I have no further questions for this witness, Your Honor."

Choynski peered at the witness and contemplated whether to cross-examine him. Doctor Lennon had indeed been impressive. After practicing law for more than thirty years, Choynski relied on his instincts. He leaned over and whispered to his clients, then looked up at Judge Deasy and said, "Your Honor, the defense has no questions for this witness."

The birds had been quiet all afternoon, but now the clamor of garbage trucks and big metal trash containers rose into the courtroom from the open space surrounding City Hall. "Court is adjourned for the day," Judge Deasy announced, his voice rising above the din.

The drunken-driving arrest had kept Basil locked up in the Folsom jail. Reading a deposition into the record would not have the impact that testimony in the courtroom would. But it also meant that Brennan would have no opportunity to cross-examine a reluctant, possibly ill-rehearsed witness. Basil couldn't have been smart enough to figure out how to avoid perjuring himself. Brennan assumed Choynski must have concluded that Basil would not make a good witness and paid someone to get him drinking and driving and arrested for combining those activities.

"Basil makes a better appearance on paper than in real life," Choynski told Lesser and Markowitz that morning as the judge took his seat and asked Brennan to call his next witness.

"Your Honor, at this time the plaintiff would like to introduce the deposition of the defendant Basil Knoblock, the stagehand at the Strand Theater in charge of working the fly system. The plaintiff asks the court reporter who wrote down his words to take the witness stand and read his testimony to the jury."

According to the deposition, Knoblock swore that after the sandbag fell, he had examined the rope that had held it to the rigging and found it in good working order. Before the court reporter could finish reading, a well-preserved matron in a blue hat with the very popular pheasant plumage muttered to her neighbor, "I don't believe that at all. How could that be?"

Brennan stood up from the plaintiffs table and said, "We rest our case."

—⁓—

Now the defense presented its witnesses. Herbert Choynski called to the stand one George White, a carpenter who did odd jobs around the Strand Theater. He told the court that theater accidents are common: Scenery fell onto performers, electric lights short-circuited, someone came in drunk and tripped over a prop or fell down the stairs.

"Every actor knows that a theater is a dangerous place and they need to take great care," he said, puffing himself up as if he were truly an expert.

Choynski called just one more witness for the defense, Otto Von Stueben, M.D., who practiced medicine at Saint Vincent's Hospital in New York. As the witness's name was called, John Davis looked up in surprise. He barely remembered contacting Dr. Von Stueben, paying for his cross-country train trip, and having him examine Ruby. He had been full of information but short on facts. In fact, Davis had heard nothing to suggest that what Dr. Von Stueben claimed he could do was based on medical science.

"Yes," Dr. Stueben told Choynski in a thick Hungarian accent. "I treated Nellie Revell, who, after a serious spinal injury, I can't remember what caused it, was paralyzed from the waist down. For five years, she couldn't even sit up. But after months of treatment under my guiding hand, she recovered and was able to walk again."

"Is it possible that Miss Adams could also recover enough to walk again?"

"Objection!" Brennan shouted. "Calls for a conclusion on the part of a witness who, moreover, never consulted with my client."

"Actually, he has, counselor," Choynski said. "Last February. Mr. Davis asked Dr. Von Stueben to come to San Francisco to evaluate Miss Adams."

Brennan turned around and looked at Davis. Davis's face made it clear that Choynski was correct.

"Dr. Von Stueben, I'll repeat the question. Is it possible that Miss Adams could recover enough to walk again?"

"It is possible."

"No further questions."

"Mr. Brennan?" Judge Deasy asked.

Brennan remained seated as he addressed the self-important little physician. "Doctor, when was the last time you examined Miss Adams?"

"In February."

"And have you examined her since?"

"No, but—"

"Thank you. No further questions."

—◠◠◠—

The next day was Thursday, which meant that, assuming the lawyers concluded their closing arguments in the next day or two, the jury might have to convene through the weekend. In room 435, the society women and news reporters sat in the chairs they had occupied all week. Many of the women had become friendly and the daily hubbub was about where to lunch.

Brennan watched the press and spectators as they were escorted into the courtroom. Sometimes it surprised him that he was an attorney, and a well-known one at that. He remembered his father working day and night to earn enough money for his children to go to college. After graduation, his father in tears, hugged him and told him how proud he was that his son was a lawyer.

Sensing he did not need to belabor the point, Brennan kept his reiteration of the facts of the case brief. He reminded the court that Moe Lesser and Morris Markowitz were the owners and directors of the New York & San Francisco Amusement

Company, which owned the Strand Theater. As such, they were responsible for managing and maintaining the premises and all the equipment. It was their duty—it was their moral obligation, he added a bit dramatically—to keep the theater equipment in good working order.

Then he raised the most important point of the case: "Had all the equipment been in good working order that night?" he asked the jury rhetorically. "If so, why did the three-hundred-pound sandbag, a major part of the mechanism that worked the curtain, fall? Why?" he repeated. "The defense would have you believe the rope used to raise and lower the sandbag was in good condition. If that is true, why did the sandbag fall? And if the rope was in good condition, why was it not put in evidence? The defense cannot support that absurd claim because the sandbag and rope disappeared the night of the accident. The stagehand who worked that equipment—who is also being sued by my client, remember—swore in his deposition before the trial that when he saw the rope that night, after the accident, it was fine. Oddly enough, he did not make it to court this week.

"Given the facts in evidence, it is difficult to conclude that Mr. Markowitz and Mr. Lesser, as well as Mr. Knoblock, the stagehand, do not bear responsibility for this terrible accident that has left my client paralyzed.

"Ladies and gentlemen of the jury, we must turn now to compensation. We need to discuss this because Miss Adams has suffered devastating injuries and losses. You've heard from Will King how talented Miss Adams is. A major motion picture company offered her a two-picture contract. She surely would have made a career and, no doubt, a substantial amount of money in Hollywood. But now, in the prime of her life, her injuries have rendered that impossible. The accident at the Strand Theater that night left her with permanent paralysis. This affects not only her ability to work and her income but her life. She is only twenty-nine years old! She is likely to live another forty years, according to her doctors.

"She will need a nurse to attend her; she will live in pain; she will always be unable to do the normal things we take for granted. She will never dance or walk or work again. She will need to live in a building with an elevator or a home without stairs. One hundred and one thousand dollars is the least you should award Miss Adams—for her hospital bills, past, present, and future, as well as for her past and future loss of income. If she were your daughter or wife or sister, what would you do? Thank you."

Choynski cleared his throat, put his hands on the defense table, and pushed himself up. "Ladies and gentlemen of the jury, my clients, in operating the Strand Theater for over seven years, have provided the good people of San Francisco with excellent moving pictures as well as vaudevillian acts and entertainment. These good men are supporters of the community. This was an unfortunate and tragic event, plain and simple; no one disputes this fact.

"But realize this, ladies and gentlemen: A theater backstage can be a dangerous place." Choynski reminded the jury of the visit to the Strand; they had seen for themselves the hazards the backstage area contained. "Everyone who worked in the theater was aware of them." Sensing that he was losing the jury, he hurried over the next part of his argument.

"Actors must take responsibility for their own actions and exercise extreme caution when backstage in a theater. Miss Adams is a veteran performer and should be aware of this. Yes, she suffered a tragic injury, and my clients truly sympathize. But she bears the responsibility for this accident, not the defendants. She should not have been standing in the wing, looking at her reflection in the mirror; she and she alone is responsible for her injuries. The verdict should read: 'We the jury finds in favor of the defendants.' Thank you. "

Choynski regarded the jury. There was no visible reaction to his statement.

Silence fell over the courtroom, with the exception of a reporter who turned to his photographer and said, "You gotta admire the old guy. He sticks to his guns."

Once Choynski returned to the defense table, Judge Deasy looked down at the leather-bound book before him and read his instructions to the jury before they left to deliberate. "Court is adjourned."

—◦◦◦—

In the hallway, John Davis leaned against the wall. The cold marble felt good against his shoulders. He had spent much of the past week triangulating between the court, Coffee Dan's, and spending time with Ruby, and he was tired.

His love for her had not changed; if anything, he loved her more. Her spirit and determination to fight after the accident were extraordinary. He contemplated her doctor's recommendation to move to Southern California, where the warmer weather might be conducive to her comfort.

As he stood in the fourth-floor hallway, he regarded a leaded-glass window embedded with the image of a ship. It was the *San Carlos*, the first ship to sail into San Francisco Bay. He thought of the *Malahat*, returning from Vancouver with another batch of rum and whiskey that night. He'd have to drive down to Princeton-by-the-Sea to receive the new shipment.

A voice interrupted his thoughts. "John, did you listen to the broadcast of the baseball game yesterday?" Brennan asked, holding up the *San Francisco Chronicle's* sports page.

"Yes. Not as exciting as I would have thought it would be. At least Washington's pitching kept the game interesting."

"If this keeps up, they just might make the World Series!"

Just as one of the news photographers tossed a wad of paper into the air and batted it with his hand, the big oak door to the courtroom opened and the bailiff emerged. "The jury's back," he reported solemnly.

"But they've only been out for an hour!" someone said as all hurried back into the courtroom.

The members of the jury had taken most of their time selecting a foreman. He began by taking an initial vote, but as he counted the yellow slips of paper, he realized the jury was unanimous. All twelve jurors agreed the defendants were guilty on all counts.

Judge Deasy appeared surprised as he walked in from his chambers and took his place at the bench.

"Mr. Foreman, have you reached a verdict?"

"We have, Your Honor."

The bailiff took the verdict from the jury foreman and handed it to the court clerk, who read it aloud.

"We, the Jury in the case of Ruby Adams vs. the New York & San Francisco Amusement Company, find a verdict in favor of the plaintiff, Ruby Adams, and against the defendants, the New York & San Francisco Amusement Company and Messrs. Lesser, Markowitz, and Knoblock, in the sum of one hundred and one thousand dollars."

John Davis rushed out of the courtroom and

down the hall to telephone Ruby, who wept when she heard the news.

From the Pacific to the Atlantic, from the docks to the suburbs, the headlines declared Ruby Adams Wins Battle.

The plaintiff's lawyer immediately moved to file a judgment lien on the property of the New York & San Francisco Amusement Company, Markowitz, Lesser, and Knoblock.

The following Tuesday, the defendants' attorney sent a Notice of Appeal to the California Court of Appeals. It was one long sentence.

> October 13, 1925
>
> Sirs:
>
> Please take notice that the defendant New York & San Francisco Amusement Company hereby appeals to the Appellate Division of the Supreme Court of the State of California to move for a new trial by the Defendant and in the sum of $101,000, and the said defendant appeals from each and every part of the said judgment as well as from the whole thereof.
>
> > Yours, etc.,
> > Herbert Choynski
> > Attorney for Defendant
> > New York & San Francisco
> > Amusement Company

◆

Eighteen

As 1926 commenced, Ruby Adams and John Davis were still unmarried and living in a Spanish-style home in Larchmont Village, a "streetcar suburb" of Los Angeles not far from Hollywood. All Ruby's doctors had felt that she would do better in Southern California's warm climate. John had already opened a branch of Coffee Dan's on Hollywood Boulevard.

The ocher-colored house was not hard to find. Built only four years earlier, it was a one-story, three-bedroom home with large doorways and a walk-in closet in the master bedroom. It had a formal dining room, and French doors led to a lovely patio, where the couple frequently entertained vaudeville friends pursuing careers in the motion picture business. Sweet Daddy Jack was playing bit parts in the slapstick comedies Mack Sennett made at his Keystone Studios, in Edendale, an enclave near downtown Los Angeles where most of the major studios shot their films, or had before moving to Hollywood, which was rapidly becoming "the movie capital of the world."

Clara LaVelle stopped by often. No longer working in vaudeville, she had married a musician who played in the band at the famous Cocoanut Grove nightclub, in the beautiful Ambassador Hotel. It made Ruby smile to think that so many of her friends were doing well.

On South Larchmont, Ruby wasn't far from a variety of doctors, dieticians, massage therapists, and alternative-medicine providers. She had tried everything to treat her paralysis, from acupuncture to cupping, an ancient technique to mobilize blood flow via suction, until she reached the conclusion that all these techniques were just a bunch of hooey.

As a breeze from the last of the Santa Ana winds swept over the front yard, the sun cast a tangerine glow over the hills in the east. The picture studios often used South Larchmont as a set, and a production crew was setting up near the house. Ruby enjoyed watching the filming, and she was already outside, rolling the oversize wheels of her wicker chair toward the movie set, as a Lincoln Town Car pulled up in front of the house.

At first, Ruby wondered whether Charles Brennan had come to bring her a check. That pleasant thought faded as soon as she noticed that he wasn't smiling.

"Hello, Ruby," Brennan said. "You're looking well."

"You should have told me you were coming. This is a special occasion."

"Sorry I didn't call first. I have business in town and thought I would stop by. There's something we have to discuss."

"You picked an exciting day to visit. Come," she said as they crossed the driveway to the wide front porch. "Many of the movie companies use our street. It's fun to watch them work."

Brennan looked toward the street as the movie crew tussled with two big black umbrellas.

"Can I offer you a cup of coffee?" John had had a ramp built along one side of the front steps, and now Ruby rolled up to the porch and sat at a little glass-topped table, preparing to ring a bell.

"No. I'm fine, thank you. Is John here?"

"Heavens, no. He's been very busy since we got here. Today he has a meeting downtown, about filming a movie at Coffee Dan's in San Francisco next year."

Two *National Geographic* magazines were perched on the wrought-iron table, and the first few pages of the *Los Angeles Times* flapped in a brief gust of wind. Brennan removed his jacket before he sat down.

"The weather's so warm already," he said.

"Yes, we're having a warm winter. So unlike San Francisco! I haven't seen rain since we got here."

As he looked at Ruby, he could smell a hint of jasmine. She was wearing a long-waisted pin-striped dress, which reminded him of a photograph he'd put into evidence at the trial. Her color was much better, and she looked stronger and handled her wheelchair with ease. Despite everything she'd been through, she looked happy.

"I hear you are singing at Coffee Dan's."

"It started as a lark. The singer called in sick, so I stepped in...so to speak." She smiled. "How is your wife? How are things going for you in San Francisco?"

"Fine, everything's fine."

"Good." A whistle broke an awkward moment of silence, and the two watched several actors and the director scurry to their places on the street. It appeared a woman pushing a baby carriage was about to be held up by a man in a motorcar.

"What is it you wished to discuss, Charles? You said that the judgment might be deposited in my bank account next week."

Brennan turned his gaze toward Ruby. "Yes, I did, didn't I?" He sighed. "I'm afraid we have a problem."

"What sort of problem?"

"I believe I've underestimated the defendants."

"Meaning?"

Brennan watched a production assistant race down the street after one of the umbrellas. Swiftly bouncing over sidewalks and lawns, it was winning the race.

"We are having difficulties collecting the judgment."

"I don't understand. Why can't the court help us

or...I don't know, seize their property?"

"The court doesn't do that. That's why we filed a judgment lien after the jury's decision."

"I still don't understand." She said as Brennan's words tumbled in her mind.

"Let me explain." Brennan leaned forward. "Two weeks ago, Colonel Choynski dangled the five thousand dollars' insurance money in front of us. That is, they paid that much."

"That sounds like progress."

His face made clear that it was not. "They sent the five thousand dollars to my office to make us think the rest would be behind it. We were lulled into believing things were moving as planned. But...." He paused. "As you know, after the verdict Herbert Choynski filed a motion for a new trial."

Ruby nodded.

"That motion was denied at the end of December. True to form, the defense has not responded. I assumed that was a delay tactic. But I also hired a private detective to investigate the defendants' financial resources. Did you know the name of the theater has changed?"

"I heard that."

"Well, according to the tax records, the property was sold to a company named Strand Realty on June 26, 1925."

The list of assets his office had received from the New York & San Francisco Amusement Company that month had included the Strand Theater, and yet the property was in the midst of being sold. It was another example of the deceptive practices that Herbert Choynski was known to specialize in. Brennan despised the culture of deception and fraud that permeated San Francisco.

"Strand Realty? What's that?"

"A company owned by Publix. Have you heard of it?"

"Well, if this doesn't beat all. Paramount-Publix—that company is collecting theaters like postage stamps."

"Right you are."

Ruby gazed at the trucks with the Paramount logo parked on her street. She, too, marveled at the deception and greed of people with power. "What can be done?" she asked.

"The defendants and their assets have vanished. In January, the state received a dissolution notice for the New York & San Francisco Amusement Company. We are dealing with a fraudulent transfer of assets, and the original company has been dissolved."

As Ruby started to speak, he held up a hand.

"I am taking two courses of action. I am filing a new case for fraud, hoping to persuade the court that the disclosure of assets—by Markowitz and Lesser as well as the New York & San Francisco Amusement Company—was fraudulent. I'm also dealing with Paramount-Publix. In June, when it appears the transaction occurred, our case was pending, and if Publix owned the theater then, they must assume the legal responsibility. I've arranged a meeting with the lawyers for Paramount-Publix this afternoon and am requesting to see the purchase contract. I'll tell them everything, if they don't already know. Let's pray for a successful outcome."

"Is that a legal term?" Ruby teased, but Brennan could see how upset she was.

Later that day, he gave the attorneys for Paramount-Publix a thorough briefing on the case. They listened carefully and asked for time to review the court's verdict and judgment and the Strand Realty contract.

———

Few people noticed George Poultney, in a knit cap and heavy winter coat, as he arrived at the court clerk's office in San Francisco City Hall on a bitterly cold day. Those who did glance at him mistook him for the clerk who'd just been hired. He opened the door to the archive room and slipped in, closing the door behind him without a sound. The room appeared just as Herbert Choynski had said it would. He looked at his watch. It was twelve-thirty—he had thirty minutes until the records clerk returned from lunch.

Working quickly, he prowled through the shelves examining case files until, at the end of the third shelf, he found the one he wanted. The flamboyant cursive handwriting clearly noted the lawsuit was Ruby Adams vs. New York & San Francisco Amusement Company et al. Poultney withdrew the file and placed it under his coat.

Once outside City Hall, he noticed a group of men lowering the U.S. flag to half-staff, in honor of the death of Calvin Coolidge's father. Poultney looked out toward the sycamore trees lining Polk Street and smiled. Then he trotted down the stairs. When he reached the little park across the street, he stood next to a trashcan and glanced over his shoulder. Not many people were out, and those who had braved the cold were watching the flag being lowered. He ignited a match and lit the edge of the file, then held the file in the trashcan until the yellow flame grew. He dropped the file and watched it burn.

A week later, Charles Brennan received a certified letter from the attorneys for Paramount-Publix. The letter informed him that they had requested the case file for Ruby Adams vs. New York & San Francisco Amusement Company from the San Francisco Superior Court, and that the court was unable to produce it. It appeared the file was missing. Since the contract between Paramount-Publix and Messrs. Markowitz and Lesser clearly stated that Paramount-Publix was not responsible for events that occurred in the theater prior to purchase, Paramount-Publix could not be held liable for the judgment.

Brennan put on his coat and hat and walked out of his office. He opened the metal gate of the elevator and jabbed the button that said LOBBY. All that work, and not a dime to show for it.

When John Davis returned from the restaurant, it was almost eleven o'clock, and the stars were bright in the cloudless night sky. To his surprise, Ruby was sitting at the dining table, a yellow telegram and envelope on the table next to a glass of milk.

"I guess I'm just the hard-luck kid," she said with a bitter laugh. "The people that inhabit this earth never cease to amaze me."

"Darling, what is it?"

"Read this."

It didn't take long. Davis slammed the telegram onto the table. "So someone has 'misplaced' the case file. And the sale contract absolves Paramount-Publix of liability. Of course."

"Yes." She turned her wheelchair and indicated a stack of law books on a small table in the living room. "I'm done with this, John," she said. She was afraid she was going to cry, after all this time. "Done with watching unkind, cutthroat people strip people like me of my livelihood and then stomp all over the justice system, as if the law does not matter. I'm going to tell Charles I don't wish to pursue this matter any further. Enough."

◆

Nineteen

A couple of months later, just a few miles south of the Mexican border, John Davis, wearing a panama hat, was driving his newest car, a gleaming black Packard Phaeton with an impressive front grill and huge headlamps. There was no finer motorcar on the road. Davis wiped the sweat from his forehead as the sun beat down on the canvas-top convertible. A few hundred yards ahead, at the southern edge of the Sonora Mountains, lay Agua Caliente.

Agua Caliente was a resort Davis's friend "Sunny Jim" Coffroth was building. Coffroth was a boxing promoter, but with the purchase of land from the local governor in Baja California, he and several developers were opening a resort hotel, casino, and racetrack. In the decade of the Volstead Act and Prohibition, many Mexicans sold land to American developers. Americans who came to Mexico looking for alcohol and gambling could expect lavish accommodations and warm hospitality.

Ruby gazed at the prickly pears and agave plants that sprang from deep ruts left in the dry roadbed by automobiles and horse carts.

"The Indians here believe the waters that flow from these mountains have healing powers," John told her, adding, "I've arranged for warm-stone massages at the clinic, where you can soak in the healing waters."

A faint smile appeared on her face, as if she was thinking, "How many treatments will you come up with until you realize what I need is a new pair of legs?"

Just beyond a tequila distillery, two uniformed men in dark glasses waved at the motorcar to stop. There was no way to ignore them. Each man flashed a menacing smile. Ruby's mistrust of people compelled her to cover her bare shoulders with a lace shawl and put her alligator purse in the glove box.

John glanced over at Ruby. "Don't worry."

He tapped the brakes and downshifted as the Phaeton eased to a stop. He kept his hands on the steering wheel and waited for the men to approach. One of the men was carrying a tin can. While his partner waited, he walked slowly to the driver's side of the motorcar, gravel crunching beneath his heavy boots.

"Something wrong, officer?" Davis asked politely.

"Donation for the police, senor," the man said with a toothy grin.

Davis turned to Ruby as he pulled out his wallet. "Graft and payola follow us everywhere, even in the middle of the Sonoran Desert," he murmured.

"At least they don't hide it," Ruby said.

John turned back to the policeman and dropped a few dollars into the can.

"Gracias." The policeman saluted and stepped aside as the automobile lurched forward.

Securing liquor for his restaurant, Davis had visited the resort a month earlier. The hotel was designed to impress. Its architecture was something between Spanish Colonial and Moorish, all arches and domed roofs and cool walkways. All week, John had talked of nothing but how beautiful the resort was, with its low-slung white-washed buildings, red-tiled roofs, colorful gardens, and elaborate fountains. Although still unfinished, it boasted a guest register of the wealthy and politically connected. The actors Charlie Chaplin, Norma Talmadge, and her sister Connie, as well as the governors of Rhode Island and California, had already stayed at the Agua Caliente.

A mariachi band was playing on the veranda, welcoming guests to the resort.

"What do you think of that?" John asked excitedly.

"Splendid!"

The motorcar came to a halt, and John signaled

for a bellboy. He and the bellboy lifted Ruby's wheelchair from the back and positioned it near the passenger side of the automobile. Then John lifted Ruby out of the front seat as a half-dozen people stood at the top of the stairs, watching.

"You still can attract a crowd," John whispered as he gently placed her in the chair. She looked up at him and stuck out her tongue. She wondered if John had asked the hotel to build the ramp up the stairway.

At the top of the stairs, John paused to catch his breath before he guided the chair through the oversize portico.

The lobby was richly decorated with tiled mosaics and vivid murals depicting scenes of a fanciful Mexico. Ruby noted a mixture of languages— English, Spanish, and German—as the couple moved across the lobby to the registration desk. A group of gray-haired, well-dressed women were playing a spirited game of Mahjong. Just beyond them, an attractive young woman sat on the lap of a portly man in a white linen suit, laughing.

"It looks like the hotel has everything his little heart desires," Ruby murmured. Indeed, Agua Caliente was quickly becoming known as a place of utter discretion, where aristocrats and *nouveau riche*, business tycoons and celebrities could mingle and enjoy themselves. Two-thirds of the resort was complete, and the rooms in the east wing were open to a select clientele.

As they approached the desk, the assistant manager,

an ingratiating fellow with beautifully Brilliantined hair and a pencil-thin mustache, hurried over. "Buenos dias, Mr. Davis, we are expecting you. Welcome." He turned to Ruby with a slight bow. "My name is Manuel Asebes. Mr. Coffroth has extended you all the comforts you require. Here are your room keys and a guest pass to the Salon de Oro. All services have been booked at the Health Clinic. Here is a list and the time of the scheduled appointments.

"Please let me know if there is anything I can do to make your stay comfortable."

Just then a trumpet rang out, followed by a chorus of young voices singing a children's song as two couples in folk costumes danced the popular Jarabe Tapatío, better known to the guests as the "Mexican Hat Dance." Soon, Ruby joined the chorus. It was a song her mother had sung in the late afternoons when she was a child.

Asebes leaned closer to Davis and asked, "Forgive me, the woman you are traveling with, Senor, is this Ruby Adams?"

"It is."

"She is a lovely woman. I don't think she will remember me, but I met her long ago in San Francisco. Please give her this," he said, holding out a gardenia. "And tell her Manuel from the kitchen at Marquad's said hello!"

Their room was at the end of the east wing. They followed the bellboy through an airy courtyard, past the gift shop and an ivy-covered wishing well. The male cicadas were beginning their mating call as he put a key in the lock and opened the door. The room was surprisingly large, filled with light from a private patio just off the sitting room. After placing the luggage adjacent to the closet, the bellboy showed John all the lights, a map of the property, and how to ring for service.

"Please let me know if there is anything we can do for you," he said in perfect English as he placed the key on a small, carved-wood dresser. Before he left, he told them the land around Agua Caliente was still wild; coyotes and pig-like creatures called javelinas roamed the area in packs. The hotel had guards patrolling nearby, in the event that a guest wandered off the property. "Enjoy your stay."

The sun in the cloudless Mexican sky beat down on smooth brick footpaths that allowed Ruby a degree of independence in the wheelchair. From the room, she could get to the lobby, the outdoor restaurant, the clinic, and wander gardens filled with honeysuckle, or was it jasmine?

By five o'clock, the couple was sitting next to a gorgeous swimming pool, among palm trees, hibiscus, pink bougainvillea, and potted gardenias and other flowers, drinking Champagne. The sun was beginning to set.

"To us!" John said, lifting his glass. "To you, for dancing into my heart."

Ruby closed her eyes, thinking how he had stood by her over the past year. When she was at the Strand, John had been waiting for his divorce to be final. That had made it easy to put aside thoughts of marrying him. She loved this man, with his graying hair and kind eyes, who would do anything for her. She wondered if he would tire of it.

"Mmm, that young girl was full of pep, wasn't she? That girl is gone, though, just a memory. In her place is this woman so full of difficulties."

John looked at Ruby, outlined against the rose and gold sky. She had endured so much and was still so beautiful. He leaned forward and took her hand. "Yes, I loved you before the accident. But I loved you after the doctors said you would never walk again. It's your spirit I love, your wit, your enthusiasm, and yes, your joy in life. I've fed off that joy. You make me happy."

"I keep thinking...." Her eyes drifted to a young woman on the other side of the pool.

The barriers she had erected in her belief that she would be a burden to him were slowly being swept aside. The thing about love, she thought, was that it took away your pride. When they were separated for more than a week, she admitted to herself how much he cheered her. Their love had been tempered, but it could not be denied.

"I know you think you'll be a burden, confined to that chair, but I will stay by your side whether we are married or not."

She avoided his eyes. "We must have an understanding."

John squeezed her hand gently. "Whatever you say."

Ruby looked across the pool again. The woman

got up from her chair and walked over to the edge of the pool. She removed her sandals, sat down, and dipped her feet into the blue-tiled pool. As her legs created figure eights in the water, she reached out and plucked two gardenias from a glazed urn at the edge of the pool and placed them in the water.

Ruby knew John was watching her, too. She was so young and lovely. She had plunged her shapely legs into the pool and was moving them with such ease. Ruby looked over at John.

"There will be times when you will betray our relationship...." she began. He started to speak, and she held up her hand. "When you do," she looked over at the woman again and chose her words carefully, "please do it with a stranger."

For the next hour, they sat in comfortable silence, sipping their Champagne. A waiter came by and lit the bamboo torches scattered throughout the garden. The cicadas ceased their mating cries, and the pool became increasingly quiet as the bright orange sun fell into the vast Pacific.

———✺———

When Ruby awoke the next morning, John was fast asleep. She eased herself out of bed and into the wheelchair, dressed, and made her way down a brick passageway to a small gymnasium. It was still dark. She gazed at a towering minaret that seemed to point to the morning star.

Exercise was crucial to her life now. Barbells imported from Germany had helped increase her upper-body strength. When asked, she would flex her bicep muscles and admit, with a coy smile, that they were not very ladylike anymore. Thank goodness for that.

After her workout, she joined John in a patch of sunlight in the flower-filled courtyard. She found him reading a newspaper and sipping a steaming cup of coffee. He looked up and smiled. "Good morning, my sweet. I trust you slept well? You look well." She had changed into a brick-red, black, and cream shirtwaist dress, with a wide Art Deco bracelet John had bought her high on her arm.

"With the help of a sleeping pill."

"Thank God for those."

"I've been thinking," Ruby said. "I'd like to move back to San Francisco."

"Do you mean that?"

"Yes. I miss my family, I miss the city."

"I miss the city, too."

"Will you be able to leave the restaurant?"

"I can find a good general manager, and Hollywood is not that far away." When she reached for his hand, he took it gently and kissed it. "It's settled then. We'll move back as soon as I get the new Coffee Dan's running smoothly without me."

"Thank you, Grandpa." What would she do without this man?

He turned back to his newspaper. "I was just reading about a horse I want to throw some money on today. He's owned by a fellow who lives up in Ojai. Horse's name is Crystal Pennant. What do you say we go to the track this afternoon?"

John was a man who thought nothing of spending a day at the racetrack, pouring over racing forms and second-guessing his picks. The annual Coffroth Handicap was set to run at the Agua Caliente Racetrack at two o'clock that afternoon— the reason, Ruby realized, he had chosen to come to Tijuana this week. With a one-hundred-thousand-dollar purse, it was the richest all-age stakes race in North America.

"How do you know about this horse?" Ruby asked.

"Are you sure you want to know?"

She threw back her head and laughed. "Oh, for heaven's sake, forget I asked."

"Tom Mix told me about the horse. See? Nothing too scandalous. Handy Mandy is favored, but Tom likes Crystal Pennant's chances. He's seen him run." He handed her the newspaper. "Why don't you come with me? It's the seventh race. We can place a small bet."

Ruby sipped from a glass of fresh-squeezed orange juice. "What are Crystal Pennant's chances?"

"He's running against a field of twenty, and the odds are five to one."

Ruby was hesitant to venture to places she was unsure she would be able to navigate. "Have you seen the track? Do you think I can get around?"

John shrugged. "I'll go over there this morning and see. But there are always ways to get around, kid. We'll position ourselves at the rail."

She gazed across the patio at the Little Star

Fountain, and with sudden clarity said, "All right then, I do enjoy a good horserace. And if Crystal Pennant wins, I think we should marry."

———∿∿∿———

The racetrack was a short distance from the hotel, next to the casino, and attracted a wealthy crowd. Ruby closed her eyes as John pushed her wheelchair through the Jockey Club. A crowd of drunken gamblers made it difficult to traverse the room. Once past the men, they moved quickly to the betting windows.

In the long line, they discussed how much to bet. Ruby suggested they bet whatever they had in their pockets. "My luck is sure to change sometime," she said.

When they reached the front of the line, John found that two horses had already been scratched. He placed a Quinella bet on Crystal Pennant and Sun God II. A Quinella bet required selecting the horses that would finish in first and second place, though it wasn't necessary to predict in which order.

The couple made their way to the rail not far from the finish line. As the trumpet sounded and the noise of the crowd rose, John took Ruby's hand and placed the ticket in her palm.

They watched as the field of eighteen horses, all wearing brilliantly colored silks, was hustled to the post. Each horse seemed to posture and dance before being positioned in its gate. At the sound of a bell, the barrier was sprung, and the pounding of horses' hooves vibrated on the turf and shook the stands. The brilliant azures and emeralds, reds and golds of the horses' coverings soon became a multicolored blur.

Light Carbine got off the post first, followed by Redcliff, closely pursued by Rip Rap, General Diskin, Shasta Gold, and Alexander Pantages. John's picks were behind but gaining steadily. Suddenly, Alexander Pantages came from behind and was soon out in front. Entering the stretch, the horse seemed to have the mile-and-a-quarter race won. Then Handy Mandy, at two-to-one odds the crowd favorite, broke slowly, and the groan from the crowd could be heard as far away as San Diego. In a desperate drive toward the home turn, Crystal Pennant overtook Alexander Pantages. In the excitement, Ruby and John didn't notice Sun God II rapidly moving up from fifth place.

Crystal Pennant, from R.C. Fields, was the first horse across the finish line. Mire Monte Stock Farm's Sun God II was second.

Ruby felt her jaw drop and her eyes open wide. John's pick would pay a fairly large purse—almost equal to the amount the jury had awarded her. The stadium erupted as tickets torn in two filled the air in a confetti shower.

John turned to her and smiled. "The hard-luck kid just got herself a winning ticket."

—◦◦◦—

After lunch the next day, John J. Davis and Ruby Adams drove to a white-washed hacienda that had been turned into a chapel, on the edge of Tijuana. As sun streamed through ocher-colored windows, the bride and groom sat in the nave next to a statue of the Virgin of Guadalupe. A few minutes after the bell tower chimed one o'clock, John Davis and Ruby Adams were married.

San Francisco Call-Bulletin
Tender Romance Revealed
"Coffee Dan" and Bride Register as Plain Mr. and Mrs. John Davis
Under the careless cloak of its casualness, the world sometimes conceals infinity of that poignant tenderness and exalted love of which the poets have sung down through all the ages.

John Davis is Coffee Dan, the man whose café has become famous from coast to coast. And long ago, back in the early part of the decade, the little hammers that beat a merry rhythm every night in "Coffee Dan's" found a gentler refrain in the man's heart.

He loved Ruby Adams, a joyous girl whose dark beauty and exquisite grace were carrying her to fame before the footlights of the theater.

But the little soubrette's dancing feet whirled into the path of an ironic, heart-breaking destiny.

It was on a January night in 1925 in the Strand

Theater. A heavy sack of sand hurled out of the overhead stage gear. It fell like the hand of fate on the slender girl beneath and stilled forever perhaps those flashing feet.

But they had danced their way into John Davis's heart, never to leave. Through the long, pain-racked months, Coffee Dan never ceased to woo the little dancer who had become a cripple. Their love was tempered in the fires of suffering and hope that would not die.

And romance at last found its full fruition. The barriers the cripple girl erected in the belief she would be a burden to John Davis were swept aside.

Fictional Epilogue

Ruby Adams began a new career as a singer, at Coffee Dan's and on the radio. She even had a small part in the first talking picture, *The Jazz Singer*, starring the famed vaudevillian turned movie actor Al Jolson. Some scenes were filmed in Coffee Dan's.

John Davis moved Coffee Dan's to Mason Street, just off Geary below the Cable Car Theatre, after he lost his lease on O'Farrell. The slide, hammers, booze, and entertainment remained, and even after the repeal of Prohibition, in December 1933, the place maintained its reputation as the noisiest joint in town. When he and Ruby visited Vancouver one year, they toured the distillery that made the whiskey Davis had smuggled in by ship, and he was given a key to the city.

Charles Brennan and his partner got so many calls from Hollywood after all the publicity from the

Ruby Adams lawsuit, they focused their practice on the entertainment industry. Charles and Leonora moved to a big home in Pacific Heights and continued to see more plays than motion pictures.

Morris Markowitz was sued for divorce by Juliette, who got the big house in Sea Cliff. Markowitz moved to Los Angeles, where he and a business partner purchased The Garden of Allah Hotel on Sunset Boulevard. He travelled back and forth to Europe, working with the European Film Industry. In 1959, when his business partner died, he was forced to sell The Garden of Allah Hotel.

Moe Lesser continued to dabble in the entertainment industry by way of a new outfit, Golden West Amusement Company. Eventually, he oversaw the family grocery store business full-time, until his hand was caught in a meat saw and he considered suing his father's company for damages. In 1940, he was brought up on a federal tax-evasion charge but could not be found.

Herbert Choynski continued to represent the rich and shady in San Francisco until he was disbarred. His windfall from the Ruby Adams case paid for his daughter's talk-of-the-town wedding to Mortimer Fleishhacker, Jr. Remembering how Choynski's father had ridiculed the city's Bavarian Jews in his newspaper in the late 1800s, the Fleishhackers did not greet him with open arms.

Will King moved to Los Angeles and wrote scripts for Fox studios until he couldn't take the crumb bums any longer and moved back to San Francisco. He and his wife, Claire, opened a coffee shop called King Cup where he performed vaudeville routines for patrons when the clock struck eight o'clock.

Basil Knoblock worked as a projectionist in movie houses around San Francisco. He began drinking less, got married, and bought a nine-thousand-dollar home in the Ingleside District, paying in cash. His friends and family never understood where he got the money. He did better than many in San Francisco—those who invested in the stock market instead of in property. On October 29, 1929, when the stock market crashed, billions of dollars were lost, wiping out thousands of investors and leading to what became known as the Great Depression.

◆

Historical
Epilogue

Ruby Adams was never able to collect from either the New York & San Francisco Amusement Company or Paramount-Publix. She was actually married twice, but her first husband died of the Spanish flu in 1918. After she married John Davis, she had a radio show in San Francisco for many years. She divorced Davis, in 1932, when she found out he was having an affair with her best friend at the Whitcomb Hotel. When her radio show ended, she opened a cigar stand in the lobby of the St. Francis Hotel. She died in her studio apartment, a bottle of sleeping pills by her bed, in 1954. It's unknown whether her death was accidental. No audio recordings of Ruby Adams exist, but it's said that her voice was similar to that of the late Dinah Washington.

Morris Markowitz was prosecuted in 1940, for tax evasion in 1925, and found guilty on all three counts. Under oath, he confessed to hiding the money owed to Ruby Adams and detailed "the hurry-up meeting" in which Herbert Choynski had advised Markowitz and Moe Lesser to hide their assets and how to do so. He and Juliette divorced sometime after 1926. He moved to Los Angeles and, with a partner, bought the Garden of Allah Hotel, once a lavish estate with twenty-five separate villas, on Sunset Boulevard. Catering to residents such as F. Scott Fitzgerald and Robert Benchley, they owned the complex until 1959, when it was sold to Bart Lytton, owner of Lytton Savings and Loan. Markowitz and Lytton hosted a party the night before the property was bulldozed. It was said, that by midnight the pool was full of empty liquor bottles.

Moses Lesser was prosecuted for tax evasion multiple times: in 1928, in 1940, and again in 1945. The conspiracy to avoid paying the judgment to Ruby Adams was documented in the 1940 case. Lesser returned to the food-service industry and had interests in his father's grocery stores. He died at sixty-eight.

Colonel Herbert Choynski's successful conspiracy to keep Ruby Adams from collecting any money from two clients, Moe Lesser and Morris Markowitz, is documented in Markowitz's 1940 tax-evasion case. Even so, Choynski continued to practice law until two weeks before his death, of a stroke, at seventy-three. Because of his military service, he is buried in the San Francisco Presidio.

Will King left vaudeville and opened a coffee shop in San Francisco on 19th Avenue, far from the Market Street theaters.

Basil Knoblock, who lost his first wife to the Spanish flu in 1918, remarried and bought a nine-thousand-dollar home in the Ingleside district of San Francisco in 1927.

John Davis's debts and marital troubles began shortly after the 1929 stock market crash and the repeal of Prohibition. These factors combined to force him to give up Coffee Dan's, which, under a new owner, moved in 1932 to Mason Street, where it remained popular through World War II and into the 1950s. After Ruby Adams divorced him, Davis was to pay her twelve hundred dollars in alimony but failed to do so. When she took him to court, he reportedly said, "I'm broke, Judge. I'm living on money borrowed from friends." He never remarried and died, at ninety, in 1968. A local newspaper reported that he spent his last days visiting shut-ins and sharing an Irish proverb, "Tell him now," by James O'Leary.

Charles Brennan continued his law practice, focusing on the entertainment industry, until his death in 1953. As far as I know, he was not in the audience at the Strand Theater on the night of January 10, 1925.

Author's note: While this book is based on the life of Ruby Adams, it is historical fiction. I have taken a few liberties with dates. Agua Caliente Racetrack, for instance, was not completed until 1928, the first year of the Coffroth Challenge.

◆

Acknowledgmets

Many thanks to all those who encouraged me to tell the story of Ruby Adams, especially my grandmother, Mae Newsom. My relatives Tina and Judy and Walter all helped with research, family stories, and valuable feedback. Ianthia Hall-Smith and Louise Felton were early and consistent book mentors. Thank you, too, to Elizabeth Aron, Tom Parks and Audrey Ribero for your assistance.

Profound thanks to attorney Diane Tucker, in Vancouver, British Columbia, and to Patrick McGraw, M.D., for your indispensable expertise regarding law and medical issues, respectively. Special thanks to Pamela Feinsilber for her editing skill, enthusiasm, and passion.

I'd like to thank Christine Moretta, at the San Francisco History Center, in the San Francisco Main Library, and Kathy McLeisterat, at the Theatre Historical Society of America, in Elmhurst, Illinois, for hours of patient help. The American Theatre Architecture Archive, also in Elmhurst, Illinois, was another invaluable resource. Additional thanks go to the St. Francis Memorial Hospital in San Francisco.

The key that unlocked the story was in transcripts and documents related to a tax-evasion case found in the U.S. National Archives: United States of America vs. Morris L. Markowitz, April 2, 1940. In addition, I consulted hundreds of books, newspapers, and magazine articles, as well as websites too numerous to mention. Particularly helpful were the 1937 San Francisco Police Graft Report by Edwin Atherton, transcribed by Hank Chabot; *Right Off the Chest*, by Nellie Revell; *Some of These Days*, by Sophie Tucker in collaboration with Dorothy Giles; *My First Love Wears Two Masks*, by Dora Barrett and Rose Cordeiro Miller; *The Great Earthquake and Firestorms of 1906: How San Francisco Nearly Destroyed Itself*, by Philip L. Fradkin; *Hollywood's Master Showman: The Legendary Sid Grauman*, by Charles Beardsley; *William Fox: A Story of Early Hollywood, 1915-1930*, by Susan Fox and Donald G. Rosellini; *Room 1219: The Life of Fatty Arbuckle*, the *Mysterious Death of Virginia Rappe*, and the *Scandal That Changed Hollywood*, by Greg Merritt; and *The Agua Caliente Story: Remembering Mexico's Legendary Racetrack*, by David Jimenez Beltran.

◆